CHAIN SAW

Also by Jackson Gillis:

The Killers of Starfish

CHAIN SAW

A Novel

Jackson Gillis

ST. MARTIN'S PRESS

NEW YORK

Design by Robert Bull Design

Library of Congress Cataloging-in-Publication Data

Gillis, Jackson.
    Chain saw / Jackson Gillis.
      p. cm.
    "A Joan Kahn Book"
    Sequel to: The Killers of Starfish.
    ISBN 0-312-02177-1
    I. Title.
PS3557.I394C5   1988
813'.54—dc19   88-12088

First Edition

10 9 8 7 6 5 4 3 2 1

To Candida,
keeper of the cabin . . .

CHAIN SAW

ONE

THE LOG TRUCK roared into view like a runaway messenger of doom. With high-stacked logs straining against meager chains, it lurched past in a cloud of sawdust and spray of mud. Then just as suddenly it was gone, swallowed by the next curve, its diesel belch and creaking load silenced by the forest all around, and only the sweet smell of cedar and smoky wet fir was left as a reminder that this time fate had just laughed, this time her lightning bolts had missed.

"Slow down, you drunk sonofabitch!"

The bearded young driver of the rural school bus screamed at the top of his lungs. He had just turned onto the old county road, had just stopped his bus and was backing out his door when the truck roared past. He'd been listening to rock music on his portable radio and he didn't even know the truck was there until he felt its deadly suck of air and whirled to see the teetering logs overhead.

"Drunk sonofabitch!" he screamed, but the red-flagged logs and splashing wheels had already disappeared around the corner past Jamison's barn. The usual bedlam on the bus behind him quieted as some of the older children, startled by their driver's frightened anger, peered curiously out. He was running around to the front of the bus now. The Jamison girl, where was she? That's what had scared him so. The little brat never waited for him to take her across the road as she was supposed to, even though there was never any traffic on this ancient road anyway.

1

But then he saw her, running safely past the barn toward an even more decrepit house. The driver turned shakily back toward his bus.

"Who's drunk?" a boy called.

"How do you know he's drunk?"

"How do you know he's a sonofabitch?" There was giggling and growing laughter again.

"They're all drunk, that's how," the driver said, "and you want to bet his brakes aren't any good? Sure, I know those bastards; they're not even supposed to use this road anymore!"

"Who's not?"

"What road? Who's he talking about?"

They hadn't even seen it. Half of them didn't even know there had been a log truck, let alone notice how close it had come to hitting them. They'd lived in these damn wet woods for so long they thought log trucks were just part of the scenery. They thought trees were good for nothing but chopping down and cutting up and hurling into people on lonely roads. The bus driver was fresh from the city, from Seattle. "Bastard log jockeys," he said, "that's who."

"My," said a girl, "you do have a dirty mouth!" The giggling turned into a roar.

"Shut up," he said, climbing back in behind his wheel. "This time I'm going to call the sheriff. Balling an overload while drunk, that's bad enough. But passing a stopped school bus—"

"Yay, get him!"

"Follow that log, officer!"

"Charge!"

But as the driver pulled his door shut he suddenly realized: His red flasher lights weren't on. When he had stopped the bus he had forgotten to turn on its warning lights. In disgust he flipped up the volume of his radio and started turning the bus around. He just hoped none of the kids had noticed that the flashers weren't on.

"Get who?" they were still yelling over the music.

"Who was it?"

"Who are you going to sic the sheriff on?"

"Screw you," he muttered.

He didn't call the sheriff and probably never had any intention of doing so. Later on, of course, he reported everything he could remember about the episode. But at the time it wouldn't have made any difference. There was nothing the sheriff or anyone else could have done to make Fate change her mind.

Less than two miles down the road, a television repairman from Anacortes who had just finished installing a farmer's aerial bounced back out through the farmer's orchard to that same old county road, and there he decided to turn uphill instead of down.

This wasn't the repairman's usual territory, but a friend who owned the only TV shop in Sooskamack, farther along on the shore of Washington Sound, had yelled for help. Since their own business was slow today anyway and his boss said he could take the new van, the repairman was only too happy to do the job. He'd been longing to sneak that beautiful new van up into the mountains to test it on a lousy road with loose-gravel corners, try its superwide tires on autumn-slick mud and maybe even some ice. There was no open deer season in the area immediately inland from Sooskamack, so the repairman knew he would have the road practically to himself, as indeed he had so far while driving up the several miles from town along the bluffs that rose higher and higher beside the Sooska River. From here on, the road would lead through even rougher country until it finally expired in the ghost lumber town of Telford. From there he could cut south to rejoin the main highway and still get home before dark, so the repairman turned right instead of left, uphill instead of down.

He floored his gas pedal and smiled as the van started picking up speed in spite of the grade. To his left he caught glimpses of the river below, but it was mostly lost in fog or low clouds, as was the island-dotted Sound far behind him. Ahead, where the really high mountains should be, there was nothing but dripping trees and darkening sky. The hills all around were junkyards of slashed vegetation, with huge rotten stumps scattered beneath tangles of second growth evergreen and leaf-dropping alder, with an occasional brighter flash of yellow where an Oregon ash still clung to October.

And then he felt the earth shake. He felt it even before he saw the monster bursting around a corner toward him, before its air horn blasted his eardrums and its sky-high radiator swung straight toward his windshield. He thought he yelled but he had no voice, and his heart stopped beating; it was only reflex action that made his hands cramp the wheel until a screaming noise stopped and he realized it had been the sound of the log truck's brakes, and now he was skidding—oh, thank God he was skidding—while the faceless high cab swiped past, the loose end of a chain ticked his roof, and a wall of rough bark almost scraped his side windows. The huge rocking logs took a final deadly swing at him, and missed.

In blessed silence he sat motionless in the ditch, slowly realizing that he was still alive and his boss's new van was barely scratched. Somehow the dice had rolled in his favor, somehow that big wheel in the sky just hadn't stopped at his number, even though he'd been daydreaming in the middle of the road and by all rights should have been crushed to a bloody pulp.

He backed out of the ditch and drove shakily on. He sure as hell wasn't going to mention this, not to anyone, not ever.

But he did, the very next day. He told most of it to his boss and then all of it to the sheriff. And the truck driver too gave a brief statement from his hospital bed.

Because one more car came up the road that afternoon, the sheriff found, just a few miles farther along. It was a big sedan with Colorado license plates whose timid driver apparently froze at the wheel, for there were no tracks veering toward the muddier right side of the road where it came around a sharp corner, and all the driver of the log truck could do was hit his brakes as hard as he could—and maybe he hit them too hard, he later admitted, even as he tried to turn his own wheels toward the shoulder, because then he felt the awful lurch of a log slipping behind him, heard the steel crack of a chain giving way. . . .

And that was it, that was all he remembered, for he was an experienced driver who had the good sense to jump for his life, even as the truck started to roll. He landed on a steep incline and skidded another fifty feet down until a tree broke his fall and almost broke his leg. He must have lain there unconscious for some time; it wasn't until the waning moon sank in a clearing sky that he finally managed to crawl back up to the road, where Mr. Jamison came by and found him shortly after midnight.

The big sedan was found farther down in the canyon, along with some of the flying bouncing logs that had smashed it apart and turned its solitary occupant into a torn rag doll. A shaken doctor described her as a slender white woman in her late fifties who had mercifully died quickly. Her name was Marjorie Dunfield and she came from Denver, Colorado, the sheriff was reported as saying. No one in the area had ever heard of her, he discovered. Probably no one would ever know why she, of all people, had arrived at that exact place at the exact time to meet such a sudden, senseless death.

But Fate had made her choice, and Fate is a bitch.

T W O

THERE WAS A cold mist hanging over the tidal flats. The blue pickup clattered slowly over the wooden planks of the causeway. Jonas Duncan rolled down his window, sniffing a mixture of salt air and sewage, dead fish and gasoline.

"Sooskamack," said Charlie Tlulagit, beside him.

Jonas was listening for something else, leaning his head out and driving even more slowly. "I can't hear them anymore. Think they're all right?"

Charlie twisted to look through the glass into the rear of the pickup, then sank back with a laugh. "They're spooked, that's all. Hiding under their own feathers. It's those dive-bombers out there. I've seen bald eagles crap like chickens when the seagulls get after them."

"Crap like chickens, that's nice," said Jonas. In the back of his pickup in rickety crates were six large turkeys that they had picked up from an Indian friend of Charlie's near Bellingham. Even on the main highway the poor birds had gobbled up a storm but now they were finally silent. Jonas smiled as he rolled his window back up, realizing that he hadn't even noticed the screaming of the gulls. For most of his adult life Jonas had lived in southern California, where he became so accustomed to the endless roar of freeway traffic that sometimes he didn't even hear it. Now he lived on an island in Washington Sound and it was seagulls he didn't hear. Seagulls were nicer, he decided, and the mud flats smelled just fine. "Okay," he said. "Sooskamack."

Ahead were waterfront sheds and warehouses, many of them

abandoned and nearly all in need of paint. To one side were a couple of half-sinking floats with fishing boats moored alongside, mostly trollers and gill-netters. The ones with scarred woodwork, torn nets, and tattered rigging looked particularly beautiful to Jonas, for they must have just returned from Alaskan waters. Someday, he thought, if he ever learned enough about boat handling, if he ever got his own ancient trawler into good enough shape, if the salmon lasted that long . . . he smiled at the old dream; it was one of a dozen that were coming back to him since he had moved to the Northwest. "I thought this place was nothing but logging and lumber," he said. Lumberjack, that was another childhood dream.

"Used to be," said Charlie. "My father claimed when he was a kid you could smell the Sooskamack paper mill fifty miles away. That's how they knew when there was a southeaster blowing, out on the island. And he meant Vancouver Island, not ours. My father was a great liar."

"What happened to it?"

"The paper mill? Burned down, years ago. There's still a big sawmill someplace south of town that does a little business, I guess. But mostly the big trees just disappeared from these parts. Forest management, they call it. Timber harvesting. Really just clear-cutting, same as rape."

Charlie took a dim view of the Northwest's once leading industry. Charlie was a sculptor who worked mostly in wood. Charlie carefully moved birds' nests and apologized to the spirits every time he felled a tree to carve into a totem pole.

They reached the main street of Sooskamack, where there were a number of wooden office buildings and stores, but most of them needed repair and quite a few were boarded up, Jonas noticed. Nearly every sign, except those that said Tavern or Motel, needed fresh paint or a new neon tube. The shabby auto traffic was sluggish and sullen. It wasn't raining, at the moment, but the few pedestrians moved as though it were, and tired paper goblins still leered from a shop window even though Halloween had been gone for more than a week. After a few blocks the town expired into vacant lots and empty billboards and sagging barns, where only the tattered remnants of old signs whispered of better days.

Charlie glanced at his watch. "How long are you going to stop here?"

"We'll make the five o'clock ferry, don't worry. I'm looking for Maple Street."

"Better slow down. That's Larch."

"I promised Mrs. Kelly I'd say hello to some friend of hers. Somebody she went to school with once."

"Oh, it's for Mrs. Kelly!"

Jonas nodded. "She asked me a couple of days ago."

Mrs. Kelly was an elderly neighbor on the island, a widow whose daffodil farm was half a mile down the beach from Jonas's cottage. The two fattest turkeys in the back of the pickup were earmarked for Mrs. Kelly, and she would need every bit of them, for she had countless grandchildren who all seemed to show up on Thanksgiving. Charlie, of course, had known Mrs. Kelly most of his life, ever since he came to the island as a lonely small boy and she gave him his first chisel and a knife. Now she collected funny white-man stories to arm Charlie's kids with at school.

In his own short acquaintanceship Jonas had found reason to love the old woman, too. When he first came to the island, a couple of years ago, there were no welcome mats for a solitary stranger—but that was all right, just the way he wanted it, in fact. Jonas had been prematurely retired, then suddenly, tragically widowed, and when Christmas came he just wanted to be alone with his memories, or thought he did. But then Mrs. Kelly showed up on his doorstep. "Holidays are the worst," she announced. "Come along," and she hauled him off to her house, crowded with relatives and friends who were on their way to more parties. It was three days before he got back home, and somewhere in between there was even a gratefully warm interlude with a Canadian divorcee on someone's boat. When the ice-breaking holiday was over and he awkwardly tried to thank Mrs. Kelly, she wouldn't let him. It was the first of many favors for which he never seemed able to repay her. She just didn't want any damn hermits living next door, she said.

Charlie was looking puzzled. "So she asked you a couple of days ago," he said. "Nothing urgent, just stop and say hello, any old time. Only then today you got that sudden bright idea we should pick up the turkeys a week early, so we could give them extra time on the special diet. There just couldn't be any connection, I suppose!" When he saw Jonas's wry grin Charlie burst into laughter. "Old ladies," he said, "you've got to look out for them!"

It was true, of course, the diet idea *was* Mrs. Kelly's. It had been her lead-in when she phoned Jonas early this morning, her transparent excuse for urging a quicker visit to the mainland. But he didn't call her on it. He had already guessed there was more than sociability to her request that he visit Louise sometime, he even had a hunch as to why Louise might be needing a visit, and he was only too happy to oblige. Anyway, they were talking on a party line and Mrs. Kelly obviously couldn't explain the new urgency. But her voice was shaking. She sounded frightened for her friend.

Jonas braked to a stop as he noticed the number on a gate across the street. Maple Street had risen steeply and now they were in a weedy and wooded residential area. The gate was one of a pair made of wrought iron and hung from heavy rock pillars that looked like lighthouses. They stood open beside a driveway that wound up to disappear behind trees and well-pruned shrubbery. On either side of the gates wrought iron fencing stretched far in both directions, apparently to embrace an entire block of elaborately landscaped woods in which an occasional iron deer or swan was visible. High among the trees Jonas caught a glimpse of a big house that obviously overlooked the whole town of Sooskamack. Maybe it *was* the whole town of Sooskamack, once.

"Jesus Christ," said Charlie. "Who is this broad?"

"Her name is Louise. Mrs. Louise Telford."

"Telford Timber? Hey, sure, it's got to be!" Charlie reached to switch the ignition off before Jonas could turn the pickup into the driveway. "Me and the turkeys," Charlie said, "you'd better leave us out in the street."

Jonas climbed out of the pickup. He strode across to enter the driveway, then sidestepped as there was a squeal of rubber and a late-model Lincoln slid out of the trees to a stop beside him. Its driver leaned his head out the window.

"Hi, buddy. You that cop from L.A.?"

The Lincoln was muddied and dented but the driver looked

uncomfortably clean in necktie and bright-checked jacket. His cheeks were jowls, his short-clipped hair was sparse, there were broken capillaries on his broken nose.

Jonas sighed. Apparently Mrs. Kelly had been advertising him. "I was once," he said. "My name is Duncan."

The man scrambled awkwardly out of the Lincoln, belly first. He grabbed for Jonas's hand and gave his arm a friendly slap at the same time.

"Hey, no offense. Some of my best friends aren't cops." His laughter was noisily infectious. "I'm Simpson, Cal Simpson. Mrs. T, she's got ants. She told me you were coming, been waiting all day for you, I guess."

"Oh, she has."

"Well, to a widow a man's a man, even if she's pushing seventy-five. Sure, she latches on to me, every now and then. But I don't mind. Her son was my best friend, or at least I worked for him for years. This here was his car. She made me take it. I just got it back from the garage, had a valve job. Listen, everything I got in this world I owe to Mrs. T. And him, of course. *He* was a little taller than me, too."

Simpson's voice rattled on but his fading blue eyes were never still, either, taking in the angular guy with the graying sandy hair and deep voice. Jonas knew he was being measured. But for what?

"Not as much muscle in the hand as you, though," Simpson was saying. "Myron, he was sort of the drink of water type, if you know what I mean, only he never drank water."

"Myron's her son and now he's dead?"

"Six months ago, had a stroke and fell downstairs up at the old shingle mill in Telford. That's where his office was. And Mack, her old man, he's been gone a hundred years. He was older than Mrs. T, anyway." The phony laughter had left Simpson's voice. He spoke more quietly. "I know that's got nothing to do with bananas, but just so you get the picture. I'm glad you're here."

Jonas relaxed a bit. "Why?"

Simpson shrugged uncomfortably. "Well, she's all alone now, got nobody close to talk to except hired hands like me."

"Talk about what?"

"Oh, it's none of my business, Mr. Duncan. I just come over to stack in a load of firewood 'cause her gardener's laid up. I noticed she's kind of upset today, that's all."

"Wouldn't have anything to do with this, would it?" Jonas fished a clipping out of his pocket. This was the hunch he'd had, after Mrs. Kelly first spoke to him about her friend Louise. He remembered that he'd seen the names Sooskamack and Telford somewhere recently, and he dug through his old newspapers until he found this story. It said some harsh things about careless logging operations, which might be upsetting to anyone named Telford. It was a story about a woman from Denver, Colorado, who had been killed early last week when her car was hit by a Telford log truck.

Cal Simpson took the clipping and stared at it for a moment, but then he snorted disgustedly. "Christ, no, that's not even true. It wasn't a Telford truck, the driver just happened to have a couple of our sticks aboard. These big-city editors, they love to make loggers the villains, like maybe it's our fault they got paper to print on or wipe their asses with." He handed the clipping back to Jonas. "Not that Mrs. T wasn't sorry about this, you understand, but it's nothing to do with her. It was just one of those things. I wouldn't say nothing, if I was you."

So much for hunches.

"Why not?" Jonas asked.

Simpson glanced hectically back toward the house. "Christ, you really were a cop, weren't you. Well, all I know is, she canceled some meeting at the bank today and got everybody sore at her, she says. But old people need to be humored, I figure. Just 'cause she changes her mind now and then is no reason to whisper and point fingers, to get her more nurses or ship her off for embalming in some desert condo. So even if she sounds a little crazy, just keep it under your hat, know what I mean? What the hell, why bring on the vultures?"

THREE

H E R H A I R W A S silver and her eyes were black as Indian arrowheads. She was a small woman who looked tall, for she stood straight and slender in a long flowing dress. It was made of material that seemed pale blue one minute, green the next. The few pieces of quite modern jewelry that she wore, earrings and a bracelet, were silver or platinum, and they sparkled with the light of tiny diamonds. In marked contrast was an old-fashioned gold watch, a man's pocket watch, which hung from a gold chain around her neck. She held her chin high so her wrinkles were barely noticeable and her straight-nosed face was beautifully, carefully made up—almost as though she were expecting to have her portrait painted, Jonas thought, and wouldn't it be fun to try, if only he were a little better at portraits. He followed her through the large main hall of the elegant old house. She was seventy-five and she moved like a dancer. But he had already noticed that the watch on her breast was trembling and when she spoke her voice was slightly out of control.

In the brief moment of their meeting at the door, Louise Telford had looked just as sharply at Jonas Duncan. She was relieved by what she saw, his big-featured face, his still unpadded body, the fact that he was careless of haircuts but not shaving. He bore the usual scars of aging, with perhaps a few special scars of his own, but he seemed to bear them as easily as the jeans, wool shirt, and old jacket he wore, the boots that had obviously just had gobs of mud kicked off them. When he stepped inside and onto her thick Persian carpets he made no mention of it, he didn't seem to feel the least bit awkward about his attire.

"Mack always wore his tin pants and mackinaw right into the Vancouver Hotel," she said suddenly, almost giggling, "or the Empress or Olympic or Multnomah, without batting an eyelash. Oh, but you probably don't even know what tin pants are, do you?" She stopped to look quickly at Jonas. "Some people don't, anymore."

"I was born in the Northwest," he said easily. "My father wore them fishing."

"Of course, I'm sorry. I didn't mean to say that, I just happened to remember. So many men are always apologizing."

Jonas gestured quietly to a large oil portrait on the paneled wall beyond the staircase. "Was that him? Your husband?"

"Yes, Mack with a k, it was short for Mackenzie. But that's really not very good, he wouldn't sit still, he was such a huge man," she said, getting her voice slowed down a bit, trying to lower its pitch. "From the time he was twelve he swam across the river every day of his life. And the Sooska was a lot bigger, then."

"Sooskamack," Jonas suddenly realized. "That's not how the town got its name, is it?"

"Of course. Didn't you know?"

Jonas smiled. "Well, at least he let the river go first."

She laughed. With his help she was calming down but not much. "His father did it," she said, moving on again. "Just a little while after Mackenzie was born. Later on Mack returned the favor; he made a little town out of one of the logging camps and called it Joe Telford. But nobody ever bothered with the Joe, and now there's hardly anything left up there." She gestured to one of the paintings on the wall ahead of them. "That's how it looked in those days. That was my fifth wedding anniversary present."

Jonas moved closer to the landscape, which had already caught his eye. It was all swirling lines of green and gray and darker hues that would trap anyone's eyes.

"Emily Carr," Jonas said, impressed and envious at the same time. "She could put you deep inside the tall timber without painting a single tree."

"Mack went over to Victoria and bought that from her, himself. There are a couple more of hers upstairs, if you'd like to see them."

Jonas glanced quickly at Mrs. Telford. She probably knew all about his attempts at painting, too. What *hadn't* Mrs. Kelly told her? Well, the big house seemed full of things he'd love to look at more closely. Like a two-foot argillite totem pole on the table beside him that looked as good as any Edenshaw in the B.C. Parliament Building, and maybe it really was an Edenshaw. Charlie would know, Charlie was a Haida, and wouldn't he love to see and touch this. But Jonas resisted the urge to do so himself. "Not now," he said. "I haven't much time, Mrs. Telford."

"No, of course not," she said hastily. "There's tea in here."

She led him into a sitting room where there were even more paintings and other objects of art. Tea was already being set on a large cocktail table by an elderly maid who then hurriedly departed. Jonas wondered if she had been assigned the job of just watching for his arrival, just waiting with the water boiling.

"You sit over there," Mrs. Telford said, but then she gestured to another portrait. "No, wait. That was Myron, he was my only child. You can't see it as well when you're sitting down."

Jonas dutifully looked up at Myron, who was slender and a little stooped and didn't look much like his father, except for his light brown, almost amber eyes. But there was no fire in them, no command, no power. Just an apologetic friendliness, as though he were hoping the artist didn't mind his assignment too much.

"It's quite like him," Mrs. Telford said. "He got that oval face from my mother's side, that same widow's peak, even when he was almost bald and his hair was whiter than it is there. Myron was about the same age as you, I imagine."

Oh, no, Jonas thought, I can't look that dead. He sat down behind the cocktail table, on which there were several small framed photographs. He was startled to see that they were *all* of Myron, who apparently had vivid chestnut hair when he was younger, though even then he looked tired and disappointed with life.

"Look at this," she said, pushing another photograph into Jonas's hand. "That's when he was in college. He liked to play drums, he even had a little group for a while, I thought they were quite good."

Jonas started to put the photograph down but checked himself as he noticed tears trying to get into Mrs. Telford's eyes, so he pretended interest in the photograph for a moment longer while she chattered.

"Unfortunately, I didn't listen to them very often, I was always off on a trip somewhere with Mack. I was a very poor mother, you understand. Always too much or mostly too little. And of course the moment Mack discovered that his only child didn't like to climb trees and tripped on his calks, then he just ignored him. After Mack died, Myron did try to help me with the business, he ran a few things as best he could, but he was drinking by then, and now it's too late, it's all too late. . . ." She shut her lips and controlled her eyes while she steadied one hand with the other to pour tea.

All right, Jonas thought, so you're still grieving for your only child and you still think your dead husband was God. You're lonely and fragile, maybe even a little mixed up sometimes. But crazy you're not.

"Mrs. Telford," he said suddenly, "why all this stuff about Myron? I realize Mrs. Kelly has probably told you all about me, up to and including the fact I like tea. But she didn't say much about you, nothing personal, that is, like what your problems are."

"Well, of course not," she said quickly. "How could she when I haven't even told her? Actually, we haven't been particularly close until lately, Flora and I. In the years since school we never had much in common."

"So I notice. You serve these little finger things and her idea of tea is to cram everybody full of ham sandwiches and stuffed eggs and chocolate cake."

She laughed. With Louise Telford bluntness, Jonas decided, was best.

"Flora was always smarter than I," she said. "But anyway, when Myron died she wrote me the nicest letter, then she sent me some clippings from those little weekly newspapers on the islands. Now we talk to each other almost every day on the telephone."

"That's nice," Jonas said, "but you're changing the subject."

"No, I'm not! I simply want you to understand. Because after Myron's death there were quite a number of city newspapers that paid attention, and some even wrote feature articles on the history of Telford

Timber, all about the 'death of an empire,' just as though there weren't any company left at all anymore, and 'now the last of the Telfords has fallen,' just as though I were out there in the graveyard with the rest of them."

Her voice was getting out of control again. She stopped to reach for an envelope that lay on the table. "Well, over the months a good many people, total strangers, have written the nicest letters, mostly about the old days, but some of them weren't very nice. Sometimes I hate to even look at my mail. Like just recently when a poor woman from Denver was killed in an accident with a log truck and of course, at first, it was blamed on us." She handed Jonas the envelope. "So when I got this, just a few days later, I almost didn't read it."

She folded her hands tightly together while she watched Jonas examine the envelope. It was postmarked from San Francisco last Thursday, with Mrs. Telford's name printed on it by someone who didn't know her street address and didn't print very well. There was no return address. He opened it and took out the letter.

"Dear Mrs. Telford," it said in careful handwriting that looked even more childish than the printing, "I hope I'm not bothering you but I want to say I am sorry for your son Mr. Myron Telford being dead. I read about him and about you in an old newspaper. It made me cry. I am also sorry because I think maybe he was my father. . . ."

Jonas glanced up. Mrs. Telford was staring at the letter in his hands as though it were a court summons or a death notice.

"I never had a father," the letter went on. "I never knew my mother, either. But don't be sorry for me, I'm fine. Anyway, I just wanted to write and say maybe I'll be seeing you someday. 'Bye, now."

It was signed, "Julie Mapes."

"And that's it?" Jonas said. "That's what you're worried about?" Before Mrs. Telford could answer he laughed and tossed the letter carelessly aside. "Crank letters. I don't know why, but they're always called that, no matter how nutty they are. Or pathetic. Or childish. This one sounds just plain silly. How old would you say she is, ten or eleven maybe?"

Mrs. Telford looked startled. "You don't think she could be as old as . . . almost sixteen?"

Jonas spoke with sudden firmness. "For that kind of game? Of course she could. Now let's have the whole story, Mrs. Telford. Stop beating around the bush."

She did.

It was Myron, apparently, who in years past had been periodically obsessed with the idea that he had a child somewhere, a little girl whom he had never seen, a girl whose nonexistence he just couldn't acknowledge.

At one time, there was reason for Myron's belief. There was a young woman up in Telford with whom he'd been sleeping rather regularly on Saturday nights, which usually stretched into Mondays, mostly because the woman was an alcoholic and Myron never minded buying drinks. Myron was well into his thirties by then but he still felt it necessary to tell his mother that he went fishing on weekends, probably because Mack was still alive and Mack would have killed Myron if he had ever let Louise learn the truth. The young woman in Telford was a part-time bar waitress, reputedly little better than a prostitute.

But then Mack died, an event which was understandably traumatic for everyone. Louise begged her son to give up his weekend fishing so he could take her to church and otherwise spend Sundays with her in Sooskamack, and of course he did as she wanted. Myron was trying to assume a little more responsibility in the company, and that took more of his time, so he saw less of the young woman in Telford. But not enough less. About a year later, through accident and a gossipy nurse, Louise discovered that Myron had been treated in Seattle for a venereal disease.

Her first reactions were sympathy and shame. But after calling in Myron's faithful secretary, a woman named Emily Stillwell, and forcing Emily to reveal what she knew about Myron's sordid affair, embarrassment turned to anger at her son's stupidity. Louise called in the county sheriff, and without saying a word to Myron, she saw to it that the young woman in Telford was sent packing out of the state that very same day, never to return.

"I told you I was a terrible mother," she said. "It never once occurred to me that he might have really cared for her, in some strange way."

"Maybe he didn't," Jonas said. "Go on."

Yes, it was true, she continued, that Myron hadn't seemed particularly upset by the woman's sudden departure. The secretary thought he was secretly relieved.

But then a few months later, Myron got a tearful telephone call. The young woman was pregnant, she said, and it was his fault and she needed money. He sent her more than she asked for, to a post office box since she wouldn't tell him exactly where she was. She called again and said she had been sick, an abortion was impossible, she was in a hospital. He sent her more money, of course. Her next drunken call came from even farther away. The baby had been born, it was a girl who was being put up for adoption—but again the woman wouldn't say where or how or with whom, and again she wanted money and he sent it.

Jonas grunted. "This sounds like one of the oldest cons there is, you know."

"I know," Mrs. Telford said. "But at least to Myron it wasn't like blackmail. He didn't care if people heard about it. Once when he'd had too much to drink, he even started to tell *me* the whole story, and when he talked about his little daughter who ought to be bearing his name, our name, he actually cried. It was the first time I'd seen him cry since he was a small boy. . . ."

Her voice caught and she cleared her throat, but then she suddenly laughed, for apparently that's what Myron had done the next morning himself. It wasn't true, he had said, there wasn't really any kid, it was nothing but a shakedown. But when, after a year, he hadn't heard from the woman again at all, he got Emily Stillwell to hire a detective agency. They worked for some time, tracing the woman from one city to another, but they never found any trace of a child. And then they discovered that the woman had died several months before in Las Vegas.

So that was the end of the trail, and over the years Myron slowly lost his obsession, even when he drank the most. But more recently, when the doctors started worrying about his heart and he started brooding about the possibility of his own death, then every once in a while Myron would mention his daughter as though she really existed. And he made several more payments to the detective agency, so he must have had someone still searching, off and on.

"And there," said Mrs. Telford. "That's it. Myron died on the seventh of March, last spring. There were daffodils and even tulips out already—"

"All right," Jonas said quietly, "but you still haven't told me why you're so upset, right this minute, by a silly letter you got several days ago."

She took a deep breath, watching him carefully. "Because I received a telephone call late last night from Olympia," she said slowly. "It was a young girl who said her name was Julie Mapes. She said she was on her way to Sooskamack, and could she come to see me this morning?"

Jonas stared at her. "What did you say?"

"I said I was just getting over the flu." She flushed. "Well, it was all I could think of. I told her I couldn't possibly see her until tomorrow. Mr. Duncan, *why* is that letter so silly? How could she have known enough to even write it? There was never anything about a missing child in the newspapers."

"Myron talked to lots of people, didn't he?" Jonas said sharply. "If his secretary hired detectives they must have asked questions at a lot of orphanages and places. Word gets around, you get on somebody's sucker list. How did she sound on the telephone?"

"Just as rattled as I was. I'm not even sure what either one of us said. But early this morning, I phoned Flora Kelly. I'd already talked to her about meeting you—that was after I got the letter—I just wanted to ask your advice, that's all. But I didn't say about what, and of course Flora told me you were retired, you just liked to paint and fish; she didn't want to impose on you unless it was very important. But then this morning I said please, it *is* important now, and I guess I sounded frightened. Anyway, she said she'd try to persuade you to come over today and the rest would be up to me."

"Good Lord, I'm not *that* retired! Of course I'd come!" Jonas said, feeling a pang of guilt. Didn't Mrs. Kelly really understand him yet? Did he still hide his feelings so much?

He pushed his cup aside. "Only you might have done better to call the sheriff instead," he said to Mrs. Telford.

"Oh, no," she gasped. "Besides, he's not the same man anymore."

"Or a lawyer, then. You must have a lawyer. Maybe he could get a court order restraining this girl."

"No! That's making too much of it. I mean yes, I do know several lawyers, naturally. But the only one in town today is the most important one, Steven Argyle, and he's the last person in the world I'd want to explain this to."

"Why?"

"Well, he's always made fun of Myron's little family phobia, as he used to call it, for one thing. Lots of people used to make fun of Myron's ideas, when they didn't think I was listening."

Even when flustered and upset she could still be evasive, Jonas noted, not liking himself for so automatically noticing such things. He smiled. "You mean you don't want Argyle to think you're getting obsessive on the same subject?"

She laughed. "But I'm not! That's ridiculous. Just because I receive a letter and a telephone call from some girl doesn't mean I take what she says seriously!"

"But you're afraid Argyle might not believe you when you say that?"

She flushed. "Of course he'd believe me! Steven's not like some others, thank heavens. He just might not take *her* seriously enough, that's all. I don't want to be unkind to the poor girl, whoever she is. You know how children make up stories about who their real parents might be."

"And always pick people who are rich or important," Jonas said dryly, rising. "Mrs. Telford, there's only one problem. I've never been licensed as an investigator in the state of Washington, so I can't really do much except give you advice."

She looked anxiously up at him. "Yes, that's mostly what I want," she pleaded quickly, "but I thought you might be willing to stay here, or come back in the morning . . . I thought if you could just be here when I talk to the girl; that's why I told her she mustn't telephone again before noon tomorrow—I felt I just had to have someone—"

"I'd rather talk to her alone, Mrs. Telford. And if I handled this, there's something else you might not like: The very first thing I'd do is go meet your lawyer, show him this letter—"

"All right. That's fine. Whatever you say!"

Jonas stopped. "Do you really mean that?"

"Of course. Don't you understand? If you tell him, it's different than if I do. He'll respect you and it will all seem *sensible*. You've been a police lieutenant in Los Angeles, you know about these things. It's not as though I'd just asked some ordinary person—" She checked herself with a sudden smile. "Well, I certainly can't ask anyone around here. Do you know I barely mentioned the subject of Myron's daughter to a man named Simpson this afternoon, and he looked at me as though I'd suddenly gone insane?" Her pleading voice was rising and trembling; she was beginning to look older than seventy-five. "Well, I am not insane, Mr. Duncan. I am not obsessed by anything. I am not talking about this the way my son did. No, and I don't need a pill, or a nap, either. I know exactly what I am doing. In asking for your help and advice, *I've* been sensible, I know I have, it's the most sensible thing I've done!"

Jonas reached to take hold of her hand. Her outburst stopped abruptly.

"Mrs. Telford," he said gently, "of course I'm going to help you. I'll be back first thing in the morning. But I was mostly in homicide, you understand, not bunco or missing persons. So if this girl turns out to be more than just a nuisance, if she really needs to be traced or investigated, then I'll have to find you someone more qualified."

She nodded and dropped her head to kiss the back of his hand before he could pull it away. She rose quickly, blinking back tears, trying to be the dancer again and not succeeding.

"Thank you," she whispered. "That's all I could ask."

She gave him the letter, and as they walked out to the front door she told him where he could find the lawyer, Steven Argyle. She would call Steven to say that Jonas would drop by for a moment on his way to the ferry.

In the doorway Jonas gave her one final curious glance, wondering how much she *hadn't* told him. But this was obviously no time to press her, and maybe he didn't need to know anyway. The favor she asked seemed simple enough. He nodded good-bye and she shut the door.

Jonas trotted down the wide brick steps, down the long driveway, and across the street to where the pickup and the turkeys were waiting.

Charlie wasn't there.

FOUR

"CHARLIE?"

No answer. Jonas reached into the pickup and tapped on its horn, but that only set the turkeys to gobbling loud enough to scare the whole neighborhood. He shooed a sniffing dog away from a tire and walked up Maple Street, thinking Charlie had probably just got out of the truck to stretch his legs, or maybe he had to take a leak. There were lots of handy places in the next block, which was nothing but woods, but Charlie was nowhere in sight. Jonas moved more rapidly in the other direction, downhill, back toward town. Surely Charlie wouldn't have been so delicate as to have gone looking for a service station. But maybe he got thirsty. Maybe he went looking for a beer.

Jonas heard sharp barking from more dogs and veered into a side street that was nothing but a rutted dirt lane leading past an empty barn. There Charlie came into view with a yapping mongrel escort, walking slowly, holding a handkerchief to his face.

"What the hell?"

Charlie had a bloody nose. The nose was swelling, and so was an ugly bruise that ran up to his eye. "You should see the other guy," he mumbled. "Not a scratch on him."

"So what did you do," said Jonas, "go down to some fisherman's bar and start explaining why the Indians should get all the salmon in Washington instead of just half?"

"Insults. Is that what I get for defending your worldly goods? He was a big blond mother, too, with a baseball moustache."

While they moved back toward the pickup, Charlie explained that he had just got out of the car to stretch a little. He was intrigued by the iron statuary he could see through Mrs. Telford's fence, and spent ten minutes or so wandering around the block admiring the rest of her landscaping. When he came back, he saw a young man beside the pickup who wasn't just a turkey fancier, for he was leaning into the cab, checking the contents of the dash compartment and looking at the car's registration. Charlie made the mistake of grabbing the guy's arm from behind, and the next thing he knew he was lying in the street while the guy ran off. Charlie picked himself up and gave chase, but then the guy turned into an alley where a van was parked. He piled into it and burned rubber, nearly running over Charlie as he tore out of the alley and away.

"It was a Dodge, I think," Charlie said, "with a blue lake and some mountains painted all over the side. Lousy colors."

They reached the pickup and Jonas checked the dash compartment, but nothing was missing. "How about the license?" he said.

"Out of state," Charlie said. "That's all I had time to see. But it wasn't California." There were so many California plates in the Northwest that their colors were as familiar as Washington's. "Hey, I think I stopped bleeding. Anyway, there was somebody else in the van, listening to a radio. I could see feet on the windshield. A girl's feet, or a kid with long hair."

Jonas glanced at his watch and with sudden decision climbed into the pickup to start the engine. Charlie scrambled curiously in after him.

"If you burn a little rubber yourself you can still catch the five o'clock ferry," Jonas said.

"*I* can?"

"You're going to drop me off downtown. If I don't pick up a rental car I can always hitch a ride to the ferry landing."

"Jonas, we can take the later ferry—"

"I'm going to stay here tonight."

"Why? What's the lady's big problem?"

"It's maybe not so big," Jonas said. "But apparently it can't wait."

He drove the few blocks into town, spotted the office building he was looking for, and stopped in front of it. Among the usual muddy trucks and battered cars parked on the street was a shiny new Rolls Royce.

"Jesus!" Charlie whispered. "Why don't you just park here? I really don't mind sticking around."

"The turkeys would. Get going." Jonas slid out from behind the wheel.

"Okay," sighed Charlie. "Only don't always go digging in these woods alone. Just remember, there's crawly things underneath."

Jonas watched him drive off, then strolled along the sidewalk, angling slowly around the Rolls. He noticed that a few other passersby did the same thing, coming close but not too close, as though afraid they might get it dirty. But most people paid no attention at all, so it probably belonged there.

The old wooden building had no elevator and the lawyer's office was on the third floor. It was a shabby little office, there was no sign of a secretary, but there was no doubt about who owned the Rolls Royce. Steven Argyle was a stocky man in his mid-forties, tanned and shaggy and elegant. His vest was double-breasted, his cufflinks golden gavels. He heard the door and stepped quickly out from his private office to give Jonas a firm handshake. He was closely followed by another man who might be younger but appeared slightly older, for he was clad as conservatively as an undertaker and was almost totally bald.

"This is Mr. Frame, Mr. Duncan," Argyle said. "Chris is Mrs. Telford's nephew. Among other things, he runs the sawmill south of town."

Frame stared suspiciously at Jonas through steel-rimmed glasses. For a big rawboned man his voice came out surprisingly high and thin. "What are you here for, Mr. Duncan? Where did my aunt meet you?"

"Singles club, probably," Argyle said, urging Frame toward the outer door. "Who cares?"

"You're some sort of police officer, I gather," Frame said, not moving. "There's nothing wrong, is there? She hasn't had any trouble?"

"Oh, of course not!" Argyle spoke more sharply. "Chris, I've got a speech in Seattle, and the dinner starts at seven-thirty. I'll call you tomorrow from Vancouver. Okay?"

Frame nodded stiffly in Jonas's direction and walked out. Argyle shut the door after him.

"News travels fast," Jonas said.

Argyle shrugged. "He was in my office just now, when Louise Telford phoned to tell me about you. If he caught a word or two, you don't mind, do you?"

"Not me," Jonas said, but he remembered Cal Simpson's earlier admonition. "Mr. Frame looked all dressed up. It wouldn't have been for a meeting at the bank, would it?"

"A what?"

"I understand Mrs. Telford canceled one today. It must have been pretty important."

The lawyer looked evenly at Jonas for a moment. "Not particularly. The president of the bank and I are executors of her son's estate. Louise has been ill, we're just finally getting around to straightening a few things out, that's all. So now satisfy *my* curiosity. You're catching a ferry, she said, so I know you're in a hurry—"

"I changed my mind, I'm staying over."

"Then come in, sit down!" Argyle waved Jonas into the private office. "You know, you're not as old as I assumed, Mr. Duncan. Louise said you'd been retired for several years."

"They did it to me a little early," Jonas said. "I couldn't pass a medical, had a touch of emphysema. It doesn't bother me much anymore."

"Now that you're out of the smog, you mean." Argyle opened a cupboard to reveal a well-stocked bar. "Scotch is good for that, I understand."

"It better be," Jonas said, glancing around the small office. Except for the bar, everything in it looked dingy and old-fashioned. The usual array of law books looked so worn they were probably secondhand when Argyle bought them. The logging photographs on the walls were framed in cheap drugstore frames that had lost their paint. Some of the photographs were turning brown.

"This is where I hung up my first shingle," Argyle said, handing Jonas a drink. "I try to get back once a week or so. I still have a little house up on the hill and a boat in the harbor. I'll be out more often when the steelhead start running. Cheers."

Apparently Argyle and his legal firm were based in Seattle now, with associates in Vancouver B.C. and elsewhere. Argyle did work for several of the biggest timber interests in the Northwest, but he'd got his start with Telford. "That's how I put myself through law school, working summers for old Mack. That's me, the damn fool on top of the tree there."

Jonas glanced at a photograph of a grinning high climber wielding a chain saw. "That's how I lost these," Argyle said, holding up his left hand to show that two fingers were missing. "I was a hundred and fifty feet up, rigging a spar pole, adjusting a cable around it, and I made the mistake of getting my fingers under the cable, right when a gust of wind hit the pole. Luckily I had a sharp knife on my belt. I whacked off what was left at the knuckles and dropped down almost to the ground before I passed out."

He had probably told the story a thousand times, Jonas thought. So okay, he likes people to know he's got credentials. But why me?

"From then until the time I finished my bar exams, the Telfords paid all my bills. I owe them a lot. But old ladies," Argyle said with a smile as he settled himself behind his desk, "sometimes they're not easy clients. What is it this time?"

Jonas handed him the letter and sat down in a lumpy armchair while Argyle read it, then read it again more slowly.

"I'll be damned," the lawyer finally said. "I thought we got rid of all that when Myron died."

"Has Mrs. Telford ever brought up the subject of a granddaughter on her own?"

Argyle looked sharply at Jonas. "Once or twice, I suppose, not seriously. Why? There's no such person, you know. Myron's long lost daughter was just a figment of his imagination. It was almost a town joke."

Jonas nodded. "Mrs. Telford told me the story. But the girl who wrote that telephoned her last night, and now I'm pretty sure the girl is here in town someplace. So Julie Mapes is real enough. She may take a little handling."

"Like with a boot in the ass, you mean."

"Maybe, if she's just a kook or a tramp. But even so, she could cause trouble, couldn't she? Particularly if Myron Telford's will hasn't been settled yet?"

"Oh, for Christ's sake," Argyle laughed. "Duncan, there's simply no credible claim the girl could make. I know I'm right about that. Myron himself admitted to me once, when he was very, very sober, that a daughter was just wishful thinking. He'd hired detectives and they proved it to him."

"Do you know who they were?"

"Some outfit down in California or Nevada, I think. The name is probably in his files or old checks someplace." Argyle reached for his telephone, flipped the cards of a desk index, and dialed a long-distance number. "It's Emily Stillwell who knows more about this than anyone else. She handled it for Myron, she's the one who's got all the answers."

"His secretary?"

"Until a few years ago. There wasn't any more office work here, her mother was dying, so she moved down to Portland."

The phone was ringing on the line but no one was answering and Argyle glanced at his watch. "Out to dinner, I guess. Here, if you want to try her yourself, later on." He hung up and reached for a note pad to write down Emily Stillwell's address and number.

Jonas pocketed the slip of paper and put down his empty glass. "It may not be necessary. I'll know better after I've located the girl, talked to her."

Argyle shrugged. "Don't waste too much time being polite. I can always get a cop or a court order to scare the kid away, you know."

"That would just attract attention, wouldn't it? Make more people curious? Mrs. Telford wants it handled quietly, I think. Anyway, the girl may not be in this alone," Jonas said, and he briefly explained what had happened to Charlie and what Charlie had seen.

Argyle frowned, then shrugged. "All right, so maybe she's got a partner. But if that's who it was, he doesn't sound too bright, poking around your car like that. Scarcely the type for a real con or shake-down."

"Maybe," Jonas said, rising, "but the best way to find out what they're up to is to move in first, upset their timing, spoil their act, if it is one. With a little luck maybe I can get rid of this whole thing tonight. I'm here as a personal favor and Mrs. Telford seems to trust me, so unless you've got some objection—"

"No, no!" the lawyer interrupted hastily. He jumped to his feet, reached for Jonas's empty glass, and moved to the bar to pour them both another drink. "You say the right things, Duncan. You don't know how nice it is to discover that Louise has been so sensible, turning this over to somebody like you. So if there's anything you need, money, dinner, a place to stay tonight—"

"No, thanks. But my own wheels are busy for a while. You might tell me where the nearest car rental is."

"Why bother?" Argyle fished out his keys and unhooked one of them. "Don't mind a Porsche, do you? It's at home now, but I'll tell you what: Go down this street to Mary's Seafood, say I sent you, and get the best salmon steak north of Seattle. Meantime, I'll have Pete, he's my Filipino houseboy, bring the car down and leave it there for you. That'll keep him from banging up the fenders for a while. Go on, take it."

"All right." Jonas nodded. "Thanks. But tell me about 'sensible.' Why is it so important? Isn't Mrs. Telford usually that way?"

Argyle laughed carelessly. "Of course. Oh, she's getting a little old, maybe, but she's still the sharpest woman I know. Don't let anybody tell you different."

"She's been ill, you said. Enough to delay the settling of her son's estate, I gather."

Argyle shrugged. "Myron's death upset her quite a bit, naturally. It was just hard for her to talk about those things for a while, that's all."

"What things? How much of an estate did he leave?"

"About a glass of bourbon and three cigars. Oh, there was a trust fund and some shares in the family corporation, but that all reverted to his mother, along with his debts; he had no other heirs." Argyle hesitated, finally decided: "This is confidential, you understand. But Myron Telford didn't just drink too much and flunk out of the university three times. We've discovered that after Emily left him he not only blew his own bank account, he also wrote checks on company accounts, dipped in the company till to support his various vices. That's what we've been straightening out, so nobody gets hurt."

"No wonder his mother is upset," Jonas said quietly. "And now along comes a kid claiming to be the result of one of those vices."

"If it's not one thing it's another. For years Louise had stubbornly kept the company going, mostly for Myron's sake, just hoping he might change, I guess. I haven't minded, there's nothing much left to manage anyway, and it's kept a few people working. Louise signs things and I handle a timber sale or lease for her now and then. But particularly since Myron died, other relatives like the Frames have been pushing her to sell out, drop her controlling share and go off on a cruise someplace."

"Why? They want control of the company?"

"They're crazy if they do. Anyway, Louise won't let go. She wouldn't budge until everything is straightened out the way old Mack would have wanted, until all the little ghosts are laid to rest."

"Ghosts," said Jonas. "But if there's nothing left in Myron's estate, how much is really left of Telford Timber?"

"What's *she* worth, you mean? Well, between her seventy percent, plus the house and a few other things—I'd conservatively say Louise Telford, today, is worth between thirty and forty million dollars."

Jonas swallowed his drink faster than he intended. "That could attract a vulture or two," he said.

"Ciao," said Argyle.

FIVE

THE SALMON AT Mary's Seafood was all that Argyle had said it would be. For some strange reason, Jonas had noticed, many places in the Northwest either overfried or otherwise overcooked their wonderful seafood. But not Mary. Mary cut a two-inch steak out of the thickest part of a blackmouth, a young chinook that had been caught that afternoon, and she broiled it over charcoal until the pink flesh was just barely firm. She scattered salt and a little lemon juice on it, nothing more, and it practically melted on the fork before it could even reach Jonas's mouth.

The Filipino, Pete, came into the restaurant to tell him where he had parked the car. Jonas could see it through the window and it was a Porsche, all right, about thirty-five thousand dollars' worth, or was that years ago? Pete was an amiable young man, but Jonas resisted the urge to pour him a glass of Mary's good Washington wine and pump him about his employer. Jonas hadn't known there were such things as Filipino houseboys anymore, but if Argyle had one that probably meant that Argyle was a bachelor, and he was obviously rich and successful, so what else did Jonas need to know? It wasn't important why Argyle had been so open and friendly with him. Maybe the lawyer was just naturally that way. Or maybe his nose was out of joint and he didn't want Jonas to realize it. Because of course a more interesting question was, why had Mrs. Telford appealed to an outsider? Why didn't she trust Argyle, or anyone else in Sooskamack, to do what Jonas was doing?

But all that was probably none of his business, and there was no chance to ask questions of Pete, anyway. A horn honked outside and the young man excused himself with a grin, saying he had a date tonight. He hurried out to join a blond woman who had apparently followed him here. She sounded impatient.

Jonas finished his dinner and walked outside to sit in the Porsche for a while, checking its various buttons and gadgets, getting the feel of its gearshift and making sure how all the lights worked. There was scattered fog tonight and he didn't want to make any mistakes. He finally started its engine and pulled away from the curb. It moved like a cat through cream.

He began with the one local hotel, which he discovered was nothing but a half-empty rooming house; it hadn't registered a new guest in years. Two small motels, one on the main street and one down by the river, were no help, either. They had never heard the name Julie Mapes. No girl of that age had been seen all week, let alone as one of their half-dozen guests.

He drove several miles inland to the main highway and methodically checked the few scattered, larger places. But again no luck. The motel business was seasonal in this area, most owners depending on summers and fishing seasons to bring periodic bonanzas; the rest of the time they just hibernated or went fishing themselves.

Jonas had rather expected that if the girl was planning some sort of shakedown, or even just a nuisance request for a handout, then she would have picked a place with a telephone, a modest and above all respectable lodging for her visit to Sooskamack. But she hadn't, and so Jonas set out to check the other places that were more obvious, though less smart on the girl's part: the campgrounds and trailer parks.

Only a few were still open, he discovered. The closest one was privately owned by a farmer who also let people pass through his considerable property to go deer hunting, for an extra charge. The place was well filled with campers, and each camper had at least two men in it, and each man was armed with at least two bottles. It was the wrong place entirely to go looking for an almost sixteen-year-old girl, particularly while driving a fancy sportscar. There just weren't any women there, of any kind. Nothing but hooted jokes, a lot of horn honking, loud radios, and even a wild shot or two. Jonas was glad to get the Porsche out intact.

The next place, a small state park that hadn't been closed for the winter yet, was farther out toward the Sound. There were probably a few hunters there, too, but they didn't make noise about it. Most of the parked campers and motor homes were dark, almost everyone was asleep.

Jonas drove slowly through the campground with only his parking lights on, and this time he didn't stop to ask any questions. He knew what he was looking for; it was the first thing he had looked for in every parking area he had visited tonight: a Dodge van with scenic painting on its sides. Here he spotted a Dodge, all right, but it was too dark to tell how it was painted, so he drove on for another hundred yards until he found an empty camp space where he could leave the Porsche. He turned off its engine and lights and listened for a long moment. He heard nothing but a couple of soft radios in the distance, and when his eyes were used to the darkness, he walked silently, casually back along the road as though he were headed for the washrooms.

There were trees bordering the space where the dark and silent van was parked, and after Jonas passed it he stepped off the road. The light from the washrooms was still some distance away and quite faint, but he was careful to stay on the shadow side of the trees until he was only a few feet from the right side of the van. From behind him came the sound of a washroom door opening and for a brief moment the light was brighter.

On the van was a crude rendition of a lake and some snow-capped mountains. This was the van Charlie had described, all right. The painting looked vaguely like Lake Tahoe.

Jonas stood there for several minutes without hearing any sound from the vehicle, and he was about convinced that there was no one inside it. Anyway, there was no rear window on this side, nor in the back end either, so he stepped silently out into the open, moving to the rear of the van. It was even darker there, and he had to stoop and feel with his fingers to make sure he was reading the license plate correctly. It was a Nevada plate.

"What the fuck you think you're doing?" a shaky voice said.

He rose, whirling toward the far side of the vehicle where the girl's voice came from, but checking himself in the very next second as the barrel of a gun separated itself from the corner of the van.

"Get out of here, you creep," the voice said louder. "Go on, or I'll shoot you full of holes. I will, I will, I will—"

"No, you won't," Jonas said quickly. "Take it easy." The gun's barrel was weaving and bumping against the side of the van. He could see a long ammunition clip. It looked like an old army carbine. The girl holding it, or trying to hide behind it, was weaving, too. She had long hair and was skinny in jeans and bare feet and she smelled like marijuana. There was an open door in the side of the van behind her, but that was all Jonas could tell in the darkness. He just hoped she could see his empty hands as he held them up higher than his face. "See? I won't hurt you."

"Get out of here, you creep, you old fart, I will, I will, get out of here!" She didn't seem to hear him and her frightened singsong voice was rising. He suddenly wiggled his left hand and the gun swung wildly toward it, so he took a chance and slapped hard with his right. She screamed as he hit the barrel and got hold of it. He threw a hip into her while he twisted the gun out of her hands, but it didn't knock her down. She lurched around him with a hard kick that just missed his crotch and he felt the rake of her grabbing nails across the back of his hand.

A car door slammed not far away and a man's voice yelled, "Hey, what's going on?" Another man said, "Wait'll I put my shoes on."

The girl was starting to scream again but this time Jonas got a hand across her mouth and held her motionless for a moment. "You're Julie Mapes, aren't you?" he whispered harshly. "Then shut up! I won't hurt you, Julie. Just shut up!" He gave her a final shake and let go.

She automatically kicked at his leg but her screaming stopped and she sank unsteadily back against the van. The man's voice and heavy steps were coming cautiously closer on the road. "What is it? What's wrong?"

"Nothing! It's all right, just a mistake, that's all," Jonas called back, in the calmest voice he could manage while hurriedly jerking the clip out of the gun. The clip was full and his fumbling fingers found a shell to pry out of the chamber, too. Of all the dumb stunts, nearly getting himself shot . . .

"Mistake! Jesus, buddy." The man approaching along the road snapped on a little pocket flashlight.

Jonas tossed the carbine back into the underbrush and moved quickly toward the road.

"Yeah, mine," Jonas laughed. "I didn't know there was anybody here." As he reached the man, Jonas fished out his wallet and spoke softly, privately. "I was just taking a look at the van there. It scared hell out of the kid, I don't blame her." He flipped the wallet open and partially exposed a courtesy badge, his retirement identification. It wasn't a real buzzer but in a quick view in the dim light it looked enough like one to do the trick. Jonas had never pulled this stunt before and he felt like a damn fool doing it now. But the man's friend had his shoes on and was on his way over with a stronger flashlight and probably a deer rifle, too. Anyway, the stunt worked.

"It's okay, Harry," the first man called, "I'll be back in a minute."

His friend turned back and Jonas pocketed his wallet.

"Looking for drugs I'll bet, ain't you," the man whispered.

"Could be."

"I saw that chick earlier, weaving down the road to pee. She was stoned. What are you going to do, haul her in?"

"No, no, just checking."

"Well, if there's anything I can do to help—"

"You'd better stay out of it," Jonas said firmly. "There won't be any trouble. I'll be leaving in a minute."

The man nodded and moved regretfully away. Jonas waited a moment, then walked back to the van, where he could dimly see that the girl sat huddled in the open side doorway, hugging her bare feet and shivering. He stopped several feet away from her.

"I'm sorry," he said. "I really didn't mean to scare you."

"Balls," she said. "What have you been saying over there? Who are you? What do you want?"

She sounded only slightly less spaced than before.

"My name is Duncan—"

"You could have been a bear," she said. "What if you were a bear? Didn't you ever read how bears eat up people in national parks?"

"I know, I'm just lucky you didn't pull the trigger."

"Balls," she said. "That guy you were talking to tried to feel me on the road a little while ago. I fell down, and he picked me up and tried to buy some pot off me, but there isn't any more, or any dust or anything else here, so you go away, too."

"Where's your boyfriend, Julie?"

"Who?"

"The big blond guy with the moustache."

"How do you know my name? He's not my boyfriend, he's a fart, that's who he is, and it's his own fault I found where he hid his pot. He left me all alone in the goddamn woods, didn't he, with all those goddamn bears?"

"Where is he, Julie?"

"How should I know? He went looking for a phone, only then he got talking to some head in a camper and off they went to drink beer. Oh, but me, I'm a juvenile female, I can't have any. All I get is creeps and bears."

"You mean he didn't want you to drink in public, or was that your own idea?"

"What?"

"Julie, I'm a friend of Mrs. Telford's. Can you understand? Does that mean anything to you? Telford?"

She was silent for a moment, she even stopped shivering for a moment, and then she suddenly laughed, a high-pitched giggling laugh. "What do you think, I can't hear good, maybe? You think I'm all jazzed or floaty or something?" She kept on laughing and giggling. She doubled over laughing, she beat her head against the van's door laughing.

"All right," he sighed. "We'll talk tomorrow." Or a cop will, he thought. Anybody in a uniform could get rid of this kid with no trouble at all. The chances of her causing any major problem were practically nil, she was even cheaper and more obvious than Jonas had expected, and it made him feel a little sick. He had always hated juvenile cases.

"Here," he said gruffly, reaching toward the corner of an open sleeping bag that lay beside her on the floor of the van. "Get back in the sack, for Christ's sake. You'll freeze to death."

"Get your hands off, you old fart!" she gasped, trying to hit him again.

He backed up a step, realizing that she had been crying as well as laughing.

"I didn't do anything wrong," she whimpered.

"Just blew your chances, that's all. What's the matter, afraid your boyfriend will beat you up? Julie, why did you come here, what is it you want?"

"Nothing! I didn't do anything. I didn't take anything, I didn't touch anything, I didn't even touch the fence!"

"What fence?"

"When I saw how old that lady in the garden was, I ran. So you can't do anything to me, I didn't do anything, I don't want anything, you just get away and leave me alone. Mert!" she suddenly screamed, whirling toward the road where headlights were bouncing into view. "Mert, here I am! I'm all right. I didn't do anything!"

As she ran toward the approaching lights Jonas jumped after her. They were the bright high headlights of a pickup. They weren't moving fast but they weren't slowing down much, either, and Jonas had to catch Julie with one arm to keep her from running right out in front of them.

"Mert?"

"Careful, sister," said an old man from the pickup, as he bounced on past and out of sight.

They stood in darkness again, but it wasn't the same simple darkness as before. In that brief moment of bright light Jonas had finally been able to see Julie clearly, and she had a delicate, oval face. Her long hair was rich chestnut in color and it swept back from a high widow's peak on her forehead. Her wide-spaced frightened eyes were light brown, almost amber.

She was the spitting image of young Myron Telford.

SIX

THE TROUBLE WITH freeways was that they were all the same, particularly after midnight when the cars were fewer, and trucks the size of railroad boxcars had you all alone to play with, to blind you from ahead with oily spray or barrel up behind you with blasting horns or rock you in passing or otherwise intrude on your hypnotic study of white lines and windshield wipers. In calmer interludes, even the dark blobs of roadside landscaping and the overhead flash of exit signs all looked the same, everywhere. Even on the way to Portland, Oregon.

It wasn't far, only a few hours south of Seattle, and when Jonas left Julie Mapes in the campground it was already too late to telephone the woman who lived in Portland, Emily Stillwell. Anyway, Jonas wanted to talk to the ex-secretary in person, and in a hurry, before he talked to Louise Telford or Argyle again. Maybe Emily Stillwell was the *only* one for Jonas to talk to, now. If Emily knew more than anyone else about Myron Telford's search for his mythical daughter, if she was the one who had hired detectives and received their reports, perhaps even still had some of those reports (and Jonas was sure he could tell in a hurry how accurate or slapdash they probably were), then certainly Emily would know what actual *proof* there was that Myron's daughter was only mythical. Or was it possible the girl really did exist?

And if she didn't exist, then who in hell was Julie Mapes?

Either way, the girl's startling family resemblance was going to shock and alarm some people. At the very least, it would delay the settling of Myron Telford's estate, and maybe some other decisions, too.

Whatever Julie's story was, she ought to be thoroughly investigated by a big and competent agency. So never mind who the little tramp really was, Jonas kept telling his own curiosity, all the way past Tacoma. And never mind chasing after her belligerent boyfriend just to find out where he fitted in. One man alone simply couldn't handle the complicated case this had suddenly turned into, even if he were qualified—and therein lay another reason for speeding to Portland. Cy Bridgeman lived in nearby Salem. Cy was a friend of Jonas's from the old days, now some sort of consultant to the Oregon State Police. Cy had spent most of his life in missing persons, he knew more about finding and identifying people than a whole kennel full of bloodhounds. Emily Stillwell was the key to this case, the key to the past, but Cy could help judge the accuracy of Emily's knowledge and help Jonas decide who should handle the investigation in the future.

And then Jonas could duck out. His favor was done, and at least part of his debt to Mrs. Kelly repaid. He could make his recommendations to Mrs. Telford and go back to his island and fix the broken step on his front porch. He could fish and watch football games on television and get ready for Thanksgiving with Charlie and his family and the overflow from Mrs. Kelly's. Sure, "Refer this case downtown," "Suspect a JD, dump her on the vice squad," "You're off duty, Duncan, go home."

That's what he wanted, wasn't it? So why was he already south of Olympia and still arguing with himself like two windshield wipers in the rain? Louise Telford hadn't even been honest with him, for Christ's sake.

Jonas knew she hadn't, the moment he saw the girl in those headlights. That's when he suddenly realized why Mrs. Telford had hauled out all her old photographs of Myron and made so damn sure he looked carefully at them. It simply had to be because she had already seen the girl herself, seen the family resemblance, but for some reason didn't want to admit it. Why? Why did she want to trick Jonas into making the discovery for himself?

But never mind that anymore, never mind any of it. If Louise Telford hadn't told him the whole story, then the hell with her, too. As Charlie said, just look out for old ladies.

Jonas winced as bullets of water slapped his right side window. A huge log truck, barreling downhill toward the Longview exit, was starting to creep past him in the right lane. The endless high logs that he could see in a quick glance seemed to be swaying slightly, as though they were in a race with the truck itself, and a long loose strip of cedar bark slapped like a wild whip in the wind. Jonas instinctively veered to the left, but a produce truck threw oil back onto his windshield. He swore aloud and stepped hard on the gas. He streaked past one truck and skidded around the other and left both of them far behind in a cloud of his own angry spray.

It wasn't until he noticed that the speedometer read ninety-five that he jerked his foot off the accelerator. He could almost hear laughter, Kathy's laughter. "What are you so upset about?" said Kathy's soft voice, somewhere inside him. "It's a Porsche, isn't it?"

Kathy had always wanted a Porsche, but they could never afford it. Kathy was Jonas's wife, once and forever. Kathy died in a secondhand Chevy on Olympic Boulevard.

Jonas took a deep breath and rubbed the back of his neck, trying to relax. Kathy was a dancer, too. That's what had been brushing against him like perfume ever since he first saw Louise Telford. And of course it wasn't Louise he was angry at, no matter how she had upset him. She was a frightened old woman of seventy-five, for Christ's sake, and if she had seen Julie Mapes before, so what? Maybe Louise just didn't trust her own eyesight, her own senses. Why *wouldn't* she want the opinion and help of an outsider?

So maybe it was only himself he was mad at (he suddenly wished he could tell Kathy) for not being able to do enough, for not ever buying that Porsche, for not changing the world enough. And the truth about Thanksgiving was that no matter how many people were going to be around, he would still be all alone. He would try not to drink too much.

But he really couldn't help Louise Telford any more. This wasn't a homicide, it was a research job that called for an organization. It was only proper that he get out before he did any more damage than he might have already done.

If Louise Telford was all alone, too, then he was just going to have to leave her that way.

"I'm sorry," he said to the crying windshield.

A short time later, he crossed the Columbia River bridge and picked his way through the usual freeway tangle that hid the darkened city of Portland. It was 5:00 A.M. by the time he found Emily Stillwell's house, out toward Willamette Heights.

She lived in one of a row of dignified wood-frame houses that were separated by gardens that looked bare but well tended even in the dark, even in cold November. A driveway led through a tiny porte cochere to an old-fashioned double-doored garage, so he drove around the block and came back to the house, and this time turned partially into the driveway as though using it to make a U-turn. As his headlights lit the garage doors, which sagged a bit in the middle, he could see a glint of metal inside. So there was a car in there: she was probably at home.

Jonas drove back to a main street where he found a coffee shop that was open, ate breakfast, and read his way through the *Oregonian* until it was well after seven o'clock and gray daylight crept into the city. Then he drove back to Emily's house, where nothing had changed, and parked beside a vacant lot across the street. By eight o'clock the entire area was thoroughly awake and in motion, with plenty of noise from children on their way to school.

At eight-fifteen, Jonas walked across the street and up onto the wooden porch and rang the old-fashioned twister bell that was mounted in the middle of Emily's front door.

There was no answer. He walked around to the porte cochere, where there was obviously a side door. It had stained glass panels in it, some of them clear enough for him to see that the inside of the house looked dark and quiet, even a little dusty, and again there was no answer to his repeated knocking.

Damn. That was all he needed, to drive this distance and then find that Emily Stillwell was out of town. Of course it was possible she could still be sleeping, and for a moment he thought of driving to the nearest service station to try calling her on the telephone. But then he walked on to the garage instead, to take a casual look there and in back. The garage doors didn't quite meet and he found that he was able to slip inside.

The car was a modest little Japanese two-door. It was registered to

Miss Emily Stillwell, all right, but where in hell was she, this woman who knew more than anyone else about Myron Telford's search for a child, this one person who had all the answers, the facts, the proof?

A car door slammed, out on the street, and Jonas stepped quickly out of the garage. There was a taxi parked across the end of the driveway. Its driver was opening his trunk to take out a couple of suitcases. Jonas walked toward him but then stopped as a gray-haired woman came hurrying around the corner of the house from the front door. She was a homely, nice-looking woman who was dressed in a suit that was slightly wrinkled. She wore a ginger lei around her neck.

"Miss Stillwell? I've been looking for you. My name is Duncan."

"Oh, no," the woman said, "I'm friend of hers from out of town. I just rang, but Emily's not at home, I guess. I was hoping she'd meet me at the airport. I sent her a wire."

"Her car is still here," Jonas said, gesturing toward the garage.

"Is it?" The woman looked toward the silent house with sudden worry, but then she laughed. "Oh, that just means she's using mine, then. I told her to use it while I was over in Hawaii, it's so much more comfortable than hers. Besides, in six weeks I was afraid the battery would run down. Oh, dear. You don't suppose she had trouble with it, do you?"

Jonas didn't answer. He was already guessing.

"I'm Marjorie Dunfield," the woman said. "I'm from Denver, Colorado."

S E V E N

I C E   C O L D   R A I N was falling when Sheriff Homer Hagenbaugh stepped out of the Evergreen Mortuary in Bellingham, but it was several moments before water dripping from his bristly white hair into his starched collar reminded the sheriff that he still carried his Stetson in his hand. He absently put it on his head, wondering if the rain would turn to snow tonight. It sure felt like it, and here it was only the middle of November, though of course Bellingham often got more snow than Sooskamack. It had something to do with the rain shadow from the Olympic Mountains, everyone said. Then the sheriff's foot slipped on the cracked sidewalk and that reminded him of rock salt. There hadn't been a real rock salt winter for several years, just cold snaps of a few days at a time, and then the warm southwesters would turn the snow and ice to mush again. Maybe this winter would be different, more like the old days, with weeks of good sledding for the kids and even ice skating on the bigger lakes as well as the ponds.

Behind him, Jonas Duncan was breathing deeply and studying the up and down traffic on the up and down street, thinking that Bellingham was really high in the mountains, even though freighters and fishing boats were tied up only a few blocks away. Bellingham always felt like the mountains, somehow, in spite of being right next to the Sound, and sometimes the mountains felt like they belonged in Alaska. Jonas shivered and coughed, for the rain wasn't heavy enough to clean the air of its sulphur smell from the pulp mill that occupied the center of the old town. All it did was brush the smoke and fumes from the stacks

43

back down onto the narrow wet streets and wood-frame houses and grimy brick buildings. This mill, Jonas noticed, lacked some of the nauseous authority of paper mills that he remembered from his boyhood. Changes had undoubtedly been made to improve the quality of emissions, the breathability of the air, or what was left of it. But Jonas wasn't sure the changes did much good. The smell was just different. Perfume had been dumped on a dead fish.

"Cigarette?" said the sheriff, stopping on the sidewalk.

"No, thanks," Jonas said, wishing he could say yes. No matter how deeply he inhaled the paper mill stink, it just wasn't erasing the saccharine scent of embalming fluid.

They stood waiting for a third man who had paused on the mortuary steps to button up his raincoat. The man was a dentist from Portland and he took his time with the buttons. He was an experienced professional man, a specialist who was damned if he was going to admit how long it had been since he had handled a cadaver. In truth, he had never even seen one before that had already been partially autopsied, and before that had been crushed in places, and burned in other places, and now was so cold it was frozen almost solid. But the gums in the splintered jaw still felt as fresh and slippery as chicken liver. . . .

The dentist suddenly spat into an azalea bush. There was a squeal of brakes from the street as he strode firmly out to join the others. A bearded young man in jeans and a yellow poncho was stepping out of a jeep to speak to the sheriff. He was a newspaper reporter from the *Bellingham Herald*, he said.

The sheriff sighed. "Who told you about this?"

"There's an apprentice mortician in there named Joe, he gets ten bucks for calling in anything we can use. I'm just surprised the local radio guys aren't here already. It is true her name is Emily Stillwell? She's some old maid secretary who used to work down in Sooska-mack?"

"In Telford, mostly," the sheriff said. "It's true."

"No question of it," the dentist said. "I did all three of her root canals myself."

The reporter nodded. "My editor used to know her a little, he says. He knows old Mrs. Telford, too. Everybody knows everybody around here." He glanced curiously at Jonas but no one offered an introduction. "Only how come the remains were still at Evergreen? In fact, how come you brought her here in the first place, sheriff? It's not quite your bailiwick."

"They've got the best cold storage in this part of the state."

"But it happened over ten days ago, didn't it? So how come you've been calling her somebody else all this time? How could anybody make a mistake like that?"

"Go in there and see for yourself, sonny," the dentist snapped.

The sheriff shook his head more kindly. "No, no, but she'd been partially burned, so had her purse, all we really had to go on was license plates and car registration. And then I knew we'd have to wait for Denver."

"But you told the newspapers—"

"What you guys printed wasn't exactly what I said. It seldom is."

"What about Denver?" Jonas asked quietly.

The sheriff gave Jonas a hard look, then suddenly reached to take his elbow. "Damn," he said. "Let's get out of here." A van from the local TV station was pulling up behind the reporter's jeep. "Doc, I'll send a statement down to your office tomorrow for you to sign."

"I know what you want, I'll have it ready."

"Wait a minute, sheriff," called the reporter.

"Her dentist there is the expert. I'm sure he won't mind being on TV."

The sheriff slid behind the wheel of his car. Jonas piled in beside him. A girl was running from the television van but she jumped aside as the sheriff snapped on his lights and siren. He spun the car into a U-turn. The dentist was already talking to the reporter, Jonas saw as he looked back, but then they disappeared behind the splash of traffic.

Jonas glanced curiously at Hagenbaugh. The wiry little sheriff sat very straight behind the wheel. His leathery face was expressionless and he never once took his steel gray eyes off the road ahead as he drove rapidly out through the newer parts of town, past shopping centers and wooded tracts and sign-boarded hillsides to the freeway. He had already cut the siren by then but he left his flashing lights on until the freeway traffic thinned and they had the fast lane all to themselves.

"Be a long time before I get my teeth fixed," Jonas finally said.

The sheriff grunted and relaxed a bit. "Shouldn't bother you, not with all your experience. Me, I'm just an amateur at this trade. Only took the job because the county buys me such nice cars."

Jonas doubted that. He knew that Hagenbaugh owned a fair-sized garage of his own in Sooskamack; he also knew that the sheriff had been reelected twice, in an area that was not noted for being permissive to wrongdoers.

"Anyway," Hagenbaugh said softly, "I kissed her once at a Christmas party."

Jonas looked quickly at him. The sheriff slapped the steering wheel.

"See the goddamn trouble was, that other woman, that Marjorie Dunfield, she's about the same general age and size. Only Denver said she was a widow lady who only moved there last year, so there weren't any close friends or relatives, no fingerprints, no dentist with X rays. And the place Mrs. Dunfield came from in the midwest before that—"

"I understand," Jonas interrupted quietly. "Mix-ups like that happen all the time. Tell me about Emily Stillwell."

"She was in my wife's bridge club for a while. Pretty good player except she always underbid. Never much to look at, but not a bad shape really. Sang soprano in the First Methodist Church. Had a sick mother down in Portland. Worked for Myron Telford a good twenty years, but I doubt if he ever called her by her first name. What the hell does anybody know about a single lady who spends her time admiring other people's kids and taking care of stray cats?"

"Was she honest?"

The sheriff gave Jonas a startled look. "Are you kidding? If it hadn't been for her, old Myron could have lost the family shingle mill in a crap game any day, without even knowing it. Ask Cal Simpson, he remembers. Emily Stillwell, she bossed Myron around like she was his governess. Balanced his checkbook and wiped his nose and sobered him up until he couldn't stand it any more and booted her out, I guess. Anyway, she went back to Portland to live. Or maybe there just wasn't any more work here, I don't know."

"It doesn't sound like you thought much of Myron Telford."

"He played nice drums," Hagenbaugh said. "I used to play a little saxophone, myself. We'd get together once in a while, Myron and me and a couple of others. None of that hillbilly stomp stuff, either. Real old-time jazz. That was before Myron got into the heavy drinking. But I always liked him. He was just born in the wrong time and place, that's all. People in Sooskamack used to think anybody who didn't shave with an axe was a fairy. And of course Myron's old man was bull of the woods, only Myron didn't give a damn if he never even made whistle punk."

"Did you know his mother in those days?"

"Not much. She's pretty far out of my league. But now I've got to go give her the full rundown on Emily Stillwell. In this part of the country, when anything happens to anybody who ever had anything to do with Telford Timber—"

"I already told her some of it," Jonas said. "I called her on the phone in that men's room, back there at the mortuary."

"Is that so."

"I talked to Mrs. Dunfield, too. I promised her I would. She's a friend of Emily Stillwell's from years back, when they were kids. She was expecting it, of course, what the doctor found. But she's still taking it pretty hard. So is Mrs. Telford."

"I shouldn't wonder," the sheriff muttered, looking sideways at Jonas.

"I wasn't trying to interfere, I just didn't want either one of them hearing it first on a radio or TV, that's all."

"Oh, it's fine by me! I don't mind if you do my work for me. But I do sort of like to know what the hell is going on. So let's have it. How'd you happen to meet Louise Telford? What were you doing down there in Portland, anyway?"

Jonas told him, or told him some of the high points, at least. When the sheriff heard about the letter from Julie Mapes he shrugged wryly. Like Steven Argyle, Hagenbaugh remembered Myron Telford's imagined daughter as nothing but a joke. When Jonas told him that Julie was here now, in the sheriff's own county (though he didn't mention the condition she had been in when he saw her), Hagenbaugh stopped smiling. Why hadn't Jonas called him for help? He knew how to get rid of the chippie brat, he'd boot her tail out of here so fast she'd *never* come back. When Jonas told him about Myron's photographs, and how much the girl looked like them, the sheriff frowned with a bit more concern, but then he shrugged.

"Well, that's only your opinion," he said. "I'll take a look at her myself. Anyway, it's got to be just coincidence. As I understand, Myron did a lot of checking over the years."

"You mean Emily Stillwell did a lot of checking for him," Jonas corrected. "Emily was the one who could answer questions, who knew more about such a girl, and whether she did or didn't exist, than anyone else. Only now Emily is dead."

Hagenbaugh didn't answer. His expressionless eyes were glued to the road once more.

"So I guess you might call that another coincidence," Jonas said.

"Guess I might," nodded the sheriff.

They rode silently for a moment.

"Did you talk to the driver of that log truck yourself?" Jonas suddenly asked.

"Of course I did!" Hagenbaugh snorted. "He's a big dumb Swede named Johansen, and if you're lucky and there's a clock striking, he'll tell you what time it is. Talk to him yourself. Talk to anybody you like. Look at the whole accident file, I don't care."

"Thanks," Jonas said. "Maybe I will."

"Why? What do you expect to find?"

Jonas shrugged. "I don't know. But Mrs. Telford is a pretty rich woman. Anyone with a believable claim to a relationship could take her for a lot of money. Or try to. But maybe that wouldn't have been so easy—or possible—if Emily Stillwell were still alive."

The sheriff thought about that for a moment. "Maybe," he finally said. "But nobody knew it was Emily who was dead, until just now."

"Someone might have known, don't you think?"

The sheriff glanced sharply at him. "Like someone involved in her death, I suppose."

Jonas shrugged again. "I don't know, I told you. But I don't believe in coincidences."

The sheriff suddenly tapped his siren. He zigzagged through the right lane traffic to reach a freeway turnoff. He drove through an underpass and onto a narrow paved road that led past a black lake and then up between lonely wooded hills toward the invisible cold mountains beyond.

"Where are we going?" Jonas asked.

"Show you in a minute. It won't take long." The sheriff drove almost as fast on the narrow road as he had on the freeway, but there wasn't any traffic and soon there were no more signs of habitation. He slowed down as they rounded a corner where the pavement was littered with muddy droppings from enormous tires, then followed the tracks off the road through an open gate that was adorned with bullet-holed warnings, from NO HUNTING OR TRESPASSING to DANGER, HEAVY EQUIPMENT and PRIVATE, KEEP OUT. They were on an ascending gravel logging road that rapidly degenerated into ruts and ridges of rocky mud. Hagenbaugh stepped hard on his accelerator to bounce them upward between green ochre tangles of stumps and vines that were twice as high as the car. The grade grew steeper near the top of the hill and Jonas saw the reason for their speed when they hit a greasy spring area and the light car started fishtailing. Its wheels caught just in time to get them over the crest . . .

And smack into the klaxon rush of an oncoming truck, which threw mud all over their windshield while it tipped its logs overhead in a blurry salute that Jonas couldn't even see. But he could feel the sudden push and suck of air, feel the slap of wet sawdust against the side windows and the prickling of hair on the back of his hand as he involuntarily gripped his leg. He relaxed the hand slowly as truck and logs disappeared behind them. After a moment he spoke casually, or he hoped it was casually:

"Is this the area where it happened? Where Johansen works, or worked?"

"Hell, no," said the sheriff, who hadn't even looked toward the passing truck. "The hell with Johansen, too. Did you notice the pretty blue eyes on that truck driver, though? I couldn't tell if it was a girl or a three-headed Dutchman."

It was Jonas's turn to glance sharply at the sheriff, but he didn't answer. The sheriff seemed to be enjoying himself. "That was a self-loader. You notice the fold-up crane on top of the cab?"

"I know what they are," Jonas said.

"They use them mostly for hauling toothpicks. But a stack of logs weighing only two or three thousand pounds each can still wake people up when you dump them on a crowded highway going sixty miles an hour, like I saw south of Aberdeen once. It took five ambulances to clean up the mess. Here, this is more like." They had reached a stretch of smoother road and he stepped harder on the gas, started picking up more speed.

"More like what?" Jonas said.

"That county road up the Sooska, where Emily got killed. Of course there's still a little pavement left there, but the curves are about the same radius, grade's about the same, you can hit almost the same speed."

"That's not all you can hit," Jonas interrupted hastily.

"I see him," the sheriff said, as a larger truck burst through the trees toward them like a tanker bearing down on a rowboat. Its driver was already braking and down-shifting for the hill farther on, so his drive wheels fired intermittent sprays of gravel like shrapnel. A couple of rocks flew in front of the car but the sheriff paid no attention, he merely skidded farther out onto the loose gravel shoulder while five enormous Douglas fir logs swayed fragrantly past.

"Albino, you notice?"

Jonas was busy noticing the huge slabs of wrinkled bark that were cracking loose from the logs.

"Or maybe you didn't look up past that five story radiator, let alone see who was in the cab. Well, I'll tell you the truth, Duncan, neither did I. Who does, when they pass a truck?"

A chunk of the bark fell off and bounced heavily behind them. The sheriff swung back into the middle of the road. "Only did you ever think how much tougher it is for him?" he continued. "Did you ever drive a rig that size?"

"Nothing bigger than six wheels."

"I thought so. Well, it's a lousy view. You look down on the dirty tops of cars, and once in a while if you're lucky you catch a flash of a lady's legs through a slanted windshield, but if you really look you'll land in the ditch, on a road like this. So mostly you don't even see the car tops go by. All you can think about is staying ahead of those dynamite sticks pointed at your tail. Sometimes the load's so heavy, if it shifts a quarter of an inch it feels like an earthquake. And if you're going downhill and a log starts to slide, then it's time to jump and you'd better jump fast."

"Is that what Johansen did?"

"The hell with Johansen, I told you. It's those damn trucks on TV that give everybody the wrong idea."

"It's what?"

"Always aiming at somebody. In one split second that they stretch into two minutes, the driver spots his victim coming around a corner, he turns a sixty-foot rig to point it easy as a handgun, and *pow* goes the car over a cliff. Or these hoods in a roll-bar pickup going fifty chase somebody in a parking lot, and of course the victim never knows how to jump sideways, oh, no, the truck just twists and turns and herds him like a cutting horse until he's squashed into catsup while the music goes crazy—well, horse shit! It's just not possible. If somebody comes at you around a corner like this in the middle of the road, there's just no time to turn. So if you think anybody behind the wheel of one of those railroad cars could *spot* somebody coming, and *recognize* them, and intentionally *aim* that whole pile of trees—"

His voice shattered in the roaring blast of an airhorn that nearly split their windshield. It wasn't a railroad car, it was a whole damn freight train with front wheels higher than their windows, stacked with howitzers of hairy cedar that blacked out the sky. Hagenbaugh spun his wheel and hit his brakes while hailstones of mud and sawdust crashed against the car and slipping logs screamed at each other overhead.

"Jesus Christ!" said Jonas, slamming his foot into the floorboards.

The car skidded slowly to a stop on the shoulder and for a long moment they just sat there, while the windshield wipers fought to give them back their watery view of the empty, cedar-scented road.

"Where the hell did you learn how to drive?" Jonas finally said.

The sheriff took a deep breath and grinned. "There used to be a jalopy track, down in Everett. Someday I'll show you my trophies."

"No, thanks."

Hagenbaugh started turning the car around, backing and filling on the gravel shoulder. "I only kissed her that once," he said quietly. "I was drunk, and she looked so damn lonesome. It was a dumb thing to do."

He put the car into second gear and drove back downhill at a more relaxed pace. Whatever the unhappy memory, he could put it aside, now.

"I just hope you got the idea, though," he said. "I may have made a mistake about who got killed in that car. But I sure as hell didn't make any mistake about it being an *accident.*"

He gestured to the soggy desolation all around them. "Look at the file, look at the odds. It just couldn't have been anything else!"

EIGHT

JONAS LOOKED AT the file. He looked at police photographs of tire tracks on cracked pavement and a muddy place on a road shoulder where there weren't any tire tracks but maybe should have been. He looked at photographs of Marjorie Dunfield's car, or what was left of it, scattered on a rocky hillside, and he looked at a few pieces of the car that had been brought back to the sheriff's garage in Sooskamack. The bits of torn metal and foam seat stuffing were so washed in mud and rinsed in rain that they meant nothing anymore, they were already just fossil remnants of an automobile. A report in the file by a police technician borrowed from neighboring Skagit County showed nothing of laboratory interest, anyway. The flying logs had literally smashed the car apart as it rolled down the steep canyon slope. Emily's torn body had been thrown aside amid a litter of shattered glass and fragments of crumpled chrome, close to a cluster of trees that finally halted the avalanche.

Not surprisingly, the truck suffered far less damage. It had only rolled over a couple of times, and had already been hoisted back up to the road and towed off to a larger garage in Mount Vernon for repairs; but there were photographs of it, too, and they showed nothing of interest. Jonas was a little surprised to see how complete the sheriff's investigation had been. A fireman summarized the burning that had taken place when the ruptured gas tank finally exploded. A doctor who treated the truck driver, Johansen, listed multiple cuts and abrasions.

Johansen's leg proved not to have been broken, so when he showed no further ill effects from concussion, he was released from the hospital. The Swede had been lucky, but by the time he jumped he couldn't have been going very fast anyway. His own statement said practically nothing, even in defense of his own driving.

There were more complete statements by a school bus driver and a television repairman from Anacortes. Both had passed the log truck earlier but neither accused its driver of speeding or any other irregularity. A few of the children aboard the bus remembered seeing the log truck just as they reached the county road to stop at the Jamison farm, but none of them really paid any attention. There had been a football rally that afternoon and they were still talking about it. One girl said their driver swore at the passing truck, but that didn't mean anything, he always swore at everybody. And of course both the school bus and the television van left the area going east, or uphill, so neither one passed the scene of the wreck, several miles farther down the canyon toward Sooskamack. No one else could be found who had traveled the old road that day.

There was a copy of an insurance investigator's preliminary report, and Jonas understood at least one reason why the sheriff had been so thorough, for obviously his testimony would be needed in the event of a lawsuit by relatives of the deceased. But no one had claimed even to know Marjorie Dunfield, and now Emily Stillwell apparently had no family left, either. Anyway, the investigator found no evidence that the truck driver had been negligent in any way or that his vehicle hadn't met the usual safety standards. Johansen's brakes had been serviced just a couple of weeks earlier, in Sheriff Hagenbaugh's own garage. And so the investigator took the usual easy way out and suggested comparative negligence, with the drivers sharing liability. That was the simplest way for the whole thing to be disposed of, by both carriers, and besides it matched the sheriff's own conclusions.

The woman (now known to have been Emily Stillwell) had obviously been driving her big borrowed car in the middle of the road, and when the truck driver tried to get out of her way he turned too quickly and his load started to slip.

It was inevitable, it was an accident, it just couldn't have been anything else.

Jonas wanted to look at the place where it happened, but his hours of daylight were shrinking. When they returned to Sooskamack the sheriff took him first to Louise Telford's house. Jonas had seen Louise briefly the evening before, when he dropped off Marjorie Dunfield (for Louise had insisted, on the telephone, that Mrs. Dunfield come to Sooskamack and stay as her guest until this frightening mix-up about Emily was settled). But it was a poor time to give Louise any more than a hasty summary of his meeting with Julie Mapes; even that much seemed almost too upsetting. And now today not only was the sheriff making his lugubrious official report to Louise, but reporters started showing up at the house and the phone kept ringing with sympathy calls, for of course Emily Stillwell had always been considered part of the Telford Timber family, even though she and Louise had nothing in common and hardly ever saw each other, except when Myron's troubles erupted. Clara, the elderly maid who had prepared yesterday's tea and was doing it again today by the gallon, seemed to have known Emily a bit better—or at least she sniffled whenever she came near Marjorie Dunfield, who just looked stunned and apologetic as though fate had somehow cheated in her favor and she didn't deserve to be here alive. The house was getting more and more crowded, and Louise, whose hostess glaze seemed about to crack, hadn't even started to settle details of a memorial service with the pastor of the First Methodist Church. The latter stood waiting like a gaunt blue heron in front of an impressionistic seascape, eyeing it suspiciously. The minister was a comparative stranger here, he confided to Jonas, since Louise Telford was a retired Unitarian and she never attended his bingo nights, either. But then Cal Simpson came booming in. Cal was shaken and curious about the news of Emily, but he also seemed to recognize what was needed here. He surreptitiously replaced the minister's tea with bourbon and fended the reporters away from Marjorie Dunfield with jokes and cans of beer. His presence seemed relieving to Louise, so Jonas nudged Hagenbaugh and they mumbled their way out.

It was then, at the sheriff's office next to his garage, that Jonas read through the file and looked at the pieces of the car. But it was already the middle of the afternoon, so when a deputy said that he had just seen Ollie Johansen over at a place called the Fish Trap, Jonas decided to postpone driving up the Sooska canyon road and walked alone down to the tavern to talk to the truck driver instead.

It was a moldy-looking place, smelling of stale tobacco and wet wool. It was surprisingly crowded for that time of day and for a split second after Jonas entered, surprisingly quiet. No one actually stared at the stranger, however; the all-male customers were too polite or shy or unfriendly for that, and a noisy pool game went on without interruption, a belligerent argument about the Seahawks' last football game soon regathered its steam. There weren't any obvious drunks in the place but no one was very obviously sober, either. It was a typical small-town "workingman's" tavern, only here the usual nonworkers all seemed to be off-season fishermen or unemployed loggers, or so the louder voices boasted. Jonas wondered how politely he would be ignored if he weren't white and middle-aged. The Fish Trap was probably a place where Charlie Tlulagit could lose a few teeth without even opening his mouth.

Jonas ordered a beer and asked about Johansen. The bartender nodded toward a corner where a square-built man in overalls and an army parka sat studying a cigar floating in an ash tray.

"If you're some kind of reporter I wouldn't bother him, though."

"Drunk?"

"Him? Hell, no. He's hollow."

Jonas picked up another glass of beer and walked over to the table.

"It's like they say about the fly," Jonas said. "Don't worry, he won't drink much."

The Swede looked up at Jonas and grinned.

"I thought maybe you were thirsty." Jonas sat down and quickly explained that the deputy named Al had suggested Johansen might not mind talking to a friend.

"Al," Johansen nodded, taking the beer. "I know Al."

Jonas started to say that he was also a friend of Sheriff Hagenbaugh's, but Johansen was already pointing at the cigar.

"That was the other man's, the man from TV. Too bad I spilled so much on it." He winked and guffawed.

"I don't smoke," Jonas said.

"Emily, that's all he wanted to talk about. I don't even know this Emily. Once maybe I see her, years ago, in Mr. Telford's office. So too bad. I am sorry for Emily."

"I know," Jonas said. "It was an accident, they tell me. It couldn't have been anything else."

"You bet your damn apples."

"Well, I won't ask about Emily. I won't ask you anything at all, until after you've checked on me with Mr. Hagenbaugh, or your friend Al—"

"Why do that? I don't care who you are, I don't care if you are a cop even."

"I was once, I'm not anymore."

"But I got nothing to tell." Johansen pointed a square dirty finger toward one of the pool players. "Ask Tony Pedilla questions. He turned over his bulldozer onto a whole road crew once, it killed three men. Two with kids. Sure, you talk to Tony."

"You didn't do anything like that. But I guess people have been pestering you, huh?"

"Sure. Today. You bet. You know what that man asks, from TV? He wants I would say something into his machine. What does it feel like, he says, to learn you kill this lady everybody knows? Hah! Well, I show you what it feels like."

He bent over to start pulling up a pants leg with both hands. There were scabs and bits of tape on his discolored leg.

"That must have hurt," said Jonas. "But you're getting around all right, aren't you? So how about going up there with me, some time tomorrow? Up where it happened."

"Huh?" Johansen stared thickly at him, still holding onto his pants leg.

"Just to look around, okay?"

"Why? Look around for what?"

"I don't know. I was curious about what kind of a load you had, that's all. Where you picked it up, maybe, where you'd been before, that day—"

"Oho," said the Swede, letting go of his pants and reaching for his beer. "You think maybe I drink beer while I drive, is that it?"

Jonas laughed. "Of course not."

The laugh was a mistake. Johansen banged his glass down in mid-drink.

"You damn well not!"

Jonas could feel motion slowing in the crowded room, he could feel voices lowering. But he didn't stop. He put a careless hand on Johansen's arm. "I guess I'm curious about something else, too. Like why you get mad so easy."

"Me?"

Someone laughed. Jonas could feel the bartender starting to move.

"Shut up, you bastard!" roared Johansen. "Shut up, all of you bastards!" He pushed Jonas's hand off and started to rise.

But a voice from the street door snapped, "Knock it off, Swede," and before Jonas could even turn to look, Johansen was sinking back into his seat and the bartender retreating to his glasses. Steven Argyle wore an English trench coat over a cashmere suit and a grouse-shooter's hat over his dark curly hair. He couldn't have looked more out of place, but he pushed his way closer as though he owned the joint—which he very likely might, thought Jonas.

"I didn't do nothing, Mr. Argyle." Johansen sounded like a sullen kid.

"I did," Jonas said quickly. "Forget it." Jonas was already rising, he had seen the look in the lawyer's dancing eyes.

"Come on," Argyle muttered.

As they moved together toward the doorway, Jonas noticed that several older men were nodding, "Hi, Mr. Argyle," or "Hello, Steve." But a couple of the younger ones seemed to make a grinning point of using the lawyer's first name, almost as though daring him not to like it. Argyle ignored them. But then Tony Pedilla drawled from the pool game: "Hey, Stevo? Don't tell me that dumb Swede's going to need a shyster! Not just to collect unemployment!"

Argyle paused by the door and deliberately lifted a middle finger toward Pedilla. It was his half middle finger. "Up yours, greaseball," he said.

Pedilla flushed but then laughed when everyone else laughed, and Jonas and Argyle moved quickly outside.

"What's the matter with you?" Argyle said. "Don't you get enough exercise over on that island of yours?"

The Rolls was parked across the street. They climbed into it.

"Seems to me you live a little dangerously yourself," said Jonas. He wasn't happy with the interruption. He had wanted Johansen to lose his temper, he was curious about the Swede's short fuse, though he had no idea what he might find out from it.

Argyle gestured with the finger again as he grinned. "That Pedilla's a jerk," he said. "They're all jerks in there. Not one of them can hold down a job for five minutes. They work one season flagging traffic or driving a tractor and call themselves loggers. They steal from the Indians' nets and call themselves fishermen. So things are a little slow here, right now; do you think any of them would bother to try Georgia-Pacific or Weyerhaeuser? Of course not. Because they wouldn't get hired, that's why. Not even to shovel sawdust. Not those guys."

"How about Johansen?"

"Oh, he's all right, I guess. A little nutty sometimes." As Argyle started the beautiful car he glanced curiously at Jonas. "Only why do you bother with Johansen? Can't resist playing cop?"

Jonas shrugged. "There are still a few unanswered questions," he finally said.

Argyle shot him a curious glance. "Emily's death was just an accident, you know. It couldn't have been anything else."

"That's what they say."

"Well, could it?"

Jonas didn't answer and Argyle didn't pursue it. Argyle had just come from Louise Telford's house, via the sheriff's office, he said, and he didn't have much time. He had been in Vancouver, B.C., since early yesterday, where his own office reached him with Jonas's brief message from Portland. When they phoned him today with the news that Emily's identification had been confirmed, Argyle walked out of an important meeting and drove down here as fast as he could. It was a damn nuisance, but he knew what a commotion the discovery might be causing and he wasn't surprised by the crowd at Louise's house, though the silly thing was, probably no one would have paid any attention at all if it hadn't been for Homer Hagenbaugh's stupid mistake of ten days ago.

"Don't blame Hagenbaugh," Jonas said.

Argyle looked thoughtful for a moment. He was driving out of town and across the causeway. "I wonder what Emily was doing up here?" he said. "I wonder what she was doing on that old road?"

"I thought you might have an idea," Jonas said.

But after another moment Argyle only shrugged. "Louise says you'll be back here tomorrow."

"I told her I'd stick around a day or two."

"She also says you seem to think this girl, Julie Mapes, may look a little like Myron Telford."

Jonas gestured to the road ahead. "If Julie's out here, you can decide for yourself."

Argyle nodded. It was less than a twenty minute drive to the campground, the way the Rolls took the wet curves. The lawyer wanted to get back to Vancouver as early as he could tomorrow afternoon, so the more they could attend to right now, the better. "Not that it means a hell of a lot," he grumbled, "even if she does look like him."

Jonas grinned. "I can hear you saying that in a probate court sometime, while the judge compares the girl with photographs of young Myron."

"All right, so maybe she comes from central casting. Maybe this is just a little fancier con than you figured, that's all."

"I don't know. She doesn't quite fit."

Argyle laughed. "Duncan, she isn't *anybody* until she makes a move or a claim. In the meantime, why worry?"

"In the meantime," Jonas said, "I just wish I knew more about Emily Stillwell and what *she* knew—"

"Oh, here," Argyle interrupted, fishing in vest pockets until he found a slip of paper, which he gave to Jonas. "One of the girls in my office dug this out of Myron Telford's old tax records."

On the slip of paper was written, "Blue Sage Detective Agency."

"There were a few canceled checks from recent years. We only keep those tax files for six or seven, but that's the same outfit, all right, the same agency Emily used earlier to track Myron's hippie girlfriend who died in Vegas."

"No address?"

Argyle shook his head. "It wasn't deductible, so the checks were in a bundle of discards. But they were all cashed in Carson City, Nevada."

Jonas nodded. "That's good enough. How big were the checks?"

"Smallest was seventy-five, the biggest about three hundred. Total was less than two thousand dollars. So they didn't do much real investigating, would you say?"

"They probably did a lot more in the early days. Isn't there any record you can find from then?"

"Not unless there are still some letters or files lying around in Myron's old office in the shingle mill. It's mostly been cleaned out, I think, but Chris Frame can show you, he keeps an eye on the place."

"That's up in Telford, isn't it? The same way Emily was headed when she died."

Argyle hesitated. "So what?"

Jonas shrugged. "Another coincidence, maybe?"

But again the lawyer didn't pursue it, and a short time later when they found that Julie Mapes was no longer in the campground, Argyle seemed relieved. It was one less thing to worry about today.

The van wasn't there either, of course, and neither was the elusive Mert. A woman in a neighboring space remembered seeing them leave. It was shortly after noon yesterday, she said, and the young man drove too fast. They played their radio too loud, too, so the woman never really heard anything they said to each other; anyway, she had already reported all this to a man in a sheriff's car who was out here not half an hour ago. He was an older man, a stiff little man who wore an expensive Stetson.

Naturally the woman was curious about what was going on, and even more curious about the Rolls Royce. But Argyle brushed her off with practiced ease and got back into the car. If Julie and her boyfriend were gone, that's all he cared about. Maybe she was gone for good, maybe Jonas did a better job than he realized of scaring her away, and the hell with how she looked. The real world was in Vancouver.

Before rejoining Argyle in the Rolls, Jonas walked through the ferns and dry undergrowth that bordered the place where the van had once been. He spotted only one of the discarded caliber .30 shells in the area where he had thrown them. The carbine was no longer there.

NINE

"PEOPLE WHO LIVE on islands," said Argyle, "either live in their dreams or get drunk before noon."

It was only a few miles from the campground to the ferry terminal. Jonas had taken a room in a Sooskamack motel the night before, but he needed some clothes and he wanted his own car back, so Argyle offered to drive him on out to the landing. They got there just in time to meet the usual cavalry charge of vehicles fresh off the incoming boat. "Always racing to catch a ferry, I don't know how you stand it," Argyle muttered as he wove through the multiple lanes of traffic toward the terminal building.

"You can drop me off by those phones," said Jonas. "I'll be back later tonight."

"Why not tomorrow? What's the rush?" Argyle asked, but he didn't seem to expect an answer. Actually he seemed relieved that Jonas had taken over some of the worrying for Louise, and at least a part of Argyle still remembered Emily Stillwell. "Memorial service is at noon," he said.

"I'll be there," said Jonas. "Thanks for the lift."

He telephoned Charlie Tlulagit, out on the island, and Charlie agreed to collect the things Jonas wanted from his house and meet him in Whale Harbor with the pickup. Jonas went aboard the ferry and spent the next twenty minutes in the humid glare and bedlam of the cafeteria line, waiting for a hamburger. All around him were kids from one of the island high schools who had spent the afternoon at some sort of band concert or competition on the mainland. The boys were brash or shy or noisy and the girls were aloof or giggly or ladylike or even noisier. They were all healthy and passably polite and sometimes very funny. They were exactly the kind of kids he and Kathy had talked about and planned for and secretly prayed for, year after year, but never had, not even one.

Usually such an evening ferry ride was a vicarious homecoming for Jonas, even if there wasn't any family waiting for him. Ordinarily he would have relaxed in the warmth and fun of the kids' presence. But tonight, for some reason, he suddenly resented their jostling, their senseless noise. They were all so damn lucky and didn't know it. They were all so different from Julie Mapes. . . .

He picked up his hamburger and ate it alone beside a sweating window that was black with rain outside. An hour later he walked ashore to find Charlie stomping his feet near the blue pickup, parked in the waiting line beside Whale Harbor's ancient ferry slip. There was half an hour before the last ferry would leave the island, so Jonas got Charlie to open the abandoned garage that he called his downtown studio. Charlie seldom used it except during the summer tourist season, and it was freezing inside, but the telephone was still connected. While Charlie looked around for a half-empty bottle of whiskey, Jonas called Cy Bridgeman, down in Salem.

Jonas wanted to find out what was inside Emily Stillwell's house, now that her death was confirmed and an official inventory could be made. In particular he wanted to know what was in Emily's records or files concerning her former boss, Myron Telford, and his search for a daughter. Of course, gaining full access to such records wouldn't be easy without a court order, but Cy was curious about the case too by now, and he had already been in touch with the officers who were attending to the customary sealing of Emily's house. His discreet probing hadn't yielded much, however. So far, they hadn't found any files at all, except for recipes and garden columns.

Oh, Lord, thought Jonas. Was it possible that Emily Stillwell was a perfect secretary to the end? Was it possible she never kept any personal records, and her former boss's secrets simply died with her? Or was that too going to be another damned coincidence to worry about?

He tried Carson City next. Information had a number for the Blue

Sage Detective Agency all right, but a recording said it was temporarily disconnected. After a few more wasted minutes Jonas located an assistant chief-of-police in Reno whom he'd known once, and the man vaguely remembered Blue Sage as a small but reputable mom and pop outfit, only pop had died a couple years ago. Their name was Snow and the widow was apparently still licensed, but if her phone was temporarily disconnected, that probably meant that like many older people in the high Carson Valley she took off for a warmer climate in the winter months. Jonas's friend would check with some of the boys in the state capitol and learn more, but of course like Cy's research in Portland, it would take a little time. . . .

That was the trouble. Everything took time, too damn much time. Now there was barely enough left to gulp a quick warming drink with Charlie before the ferry whistled and Jonas had to run for the pickup to drive it aboard.

"What's the hurry?" Charlie called after him. "Why not wait until tomorrow?" As when Argyle asked it, Jonas evaded answering; maybe there was no sensible answer. But when he settled himself beside a window in the almost empty ferry and watched barnacled pilings slip away into darkness, he felt sudden empathy for Argyle's distrust of islands. If your real world was elsewhere, if your worries were elsewhere, there were times when an island could feel like a trap. Until he'd explained all those damned coincidences, Jonas decided, until he knew for sure whether Emily Stillwell's death was entirely an accident, he was going to feel a lot more comfortable staying in Sooskamack.

Comfortable, he soon learned, was not the right word.

While the wind and rain whistled outside, Jonas unfolded a sketch pad that he had asked Charlie to stick in his suitcase along with other things from his house. Like every sketch pad Jonas owned, the first few pages were filled with doodles and drawings of Kathy. It was an automatic warm-up his pencil or charcoal always seemed to take, and these sketches contained some of his best remembrances of her. It was Kathy who long ago had given Jonas his first set of paints and persuaded him to try them, on the excuse that it might help him stop smoking, might give him something to do with his restless hands and nerves when he was upset about a murder case. It had never occurred to Jonas that he could even draw a line, let alone put occasional beauty onto paper or canvas. But Kathy always seemed to know more about him than he did. Jonas didn't think a cop could spare the time for lectures or concerts, either, and when the shock of his forced retirement hit him, it was Kathy who bought him a surf-fishing rod and persuaded him to move closer to the ocean. Maybe she had never managed to give him a child, but in every other way Kathy had kept expanding his whole life—until a junkie going ninety miles an hour through a red light on Olympic Boulevard ended it all forever. Or so Jonas thought, in his stunned grieving, and so did half the bartenders in Santa Monica, where formerly he had only jogged happily past on the beach. When he was finally fired from his last part-time job with a sleazy detective agency, when he finally dried out in a hospital somewhere and started remembering the cleaner air in the places of his childhood, then it was still Kathy's gifts that kept him trying, kept him moving until he got there. All those random gifts of love, and no one to give them back to . . .

Jonas turned to a blank page and went to work. It was Julie Mapes he wanted to get down on paper before he forgot, not only for himself but to show to Louise Telford and maybe some other people in Sooska-mack. Julie Mapes, exactly as he had seen her in the campground: the widow's peak and straggly hair, the wide-set eyes with their suspicious angry stare, the defensive thin shoulders, the sullen mouth. He sketched her a dozen times from half a dozen angles, full-face, profile, he even tried full figure in jeans and baggy top and torn sweater. He did his damnedest to draw the tough city kid he had seen that night.

But if there was any resemblance to Myron Telford it probably didn't show, and for some reason, Julie kept coming out like the girls in the cafeteria line. Her mouth only looked vulnerable, her eyes frightened or lonely. In one, she was even wistfully pretty.

He slammed the pad shut and stared out at a shadowy tug whose mast lights indicated a tow—a log boom, probably, for in the splashing darkness of the strait it was as low-lying as a parade of whales. Drawing the girl was a waste of time, he decided. He just wasn't that good at portraits, yet.

But someone must have appreciated them. It was eleven o'clock when he drove into the overgrown yard of the little motel by the mouth of the Sooska River. He counted to five, for there were no numbers visible on the weathered cottages, and then he turned his pickup into the next empty shed. His key fit in the cottage door, so it was his room, all right. But when Jonas reached for the light switch, someone else's hand was there.

He swung and ducked as fast as he could, but a railroad tie hit his shoulder and knocked him back against the door. The suitcase fell out of his hand and he tripped over it as he tried to lunge sideways for a leg that should have been there but wasn't. As he fell an anvil hit him in the small of the back. He twisted and grabbed for what turned out to be a boot, about size fourteen, but before he could do anything with it, his assailant's knee crashed down on his chest. The man grunted and struggled back to his feet, hauling Jonas along with him. Jonas grabbed with both hands for the arm that was hoisting his jacket—it was at least big as Paul Bunyan's arm and it had a funny lump in it near the elbow— but before Jonas could get any leverage to break the damn thing, or even get enough air back into his chest to yell at the bastard, a fist hit his jaw and the floor rose to meet the back of his head.

When he finally noticed where he was lying it was almost midnight. The room was a mess and so was his open suitcase. Two things were missing: his wallet, and the sketch pad with its drawings of Julie Mapes.

And Kathy.

TEN

For the beauty of the earth,
For the beauty of the skies,
For the love which from our birth
Over and around us lies. . . .

IT WASN'T AN UNUSUAL HYMN for a funeral or memorial service, but it was a great favorite of Emily's, the pastor announced. She particularly enjoyed singing the soprano melody, and sometimes she sang it as a solo with the choir in soft harmony. Her voice was still missed in this house of worship, even though she had moved away several years ago. Perhaps the words had a special meaning to Emily, for she had always loved nature, and never failed to share buckets of wild berries or rose cuttings or divided bulbs with the pastor's wife.

The memories of Emily were a little different from Homer Hagenbaugh's, Jonas observed, as he tried to make his sore back and aching shoulder more comfortable in the hard straight pew. But the sheriff had a good voice, a surprisingly rich bass voice, and he also sang (standing erect and expressionless) in this same small choir in the small simple church that was now crowded almost to overflowing. Jonas had tried to call Hagenbaugh early in the morning, when he woke up with a paralyzed jaw and nails in his head. But after a shower and a drink and some gingerly eaten breakfast he was glad that the sheriff hadn't answered his phone. Jonas would much rather track down his own assailant if possible; at least he could wait until after the memorial service to report what had happened.

Or maybe the bastard was right here in church. There was certainly a large enough selection of lanky or beefy or red-necked men, along with their dour-looking women. The usual forest unfriendlies, Charlie would say, but to Jonas at the moment they looked more like phonies and gossips. From their overdone reverence and thinly veiled curiosity about each other, most of those present, Jonas cynically decided, had scarcely even known who Emily Stillwell was in her lifetime. Her real friends were probably few. But in the mixed up accident of her death, Emily was a sudden celebrity, so the good people of Sooskamack had eagerly gathered to give her a respectful farewell. Why, maybe they'd even get to be on TV!

Some women were starting to cry, however, and the man in the dark suit who sat beside the minister, nervously consulting his notes for a eulogy, looked properly somber and pale. The man was Chris Frame, Louise Telford's nephew and the last close male descendant of the giants who built Telford Timber.

"Bet he could use a snort." Cal Simpson's rasping chuckle was as quiet as the big man could manage. "You shoulda heard him complain when Mrs. T put the finger on him for this, yesterday afternoon." But the whisper wasn't quiet enough, a woman behind them murmured, "Sh-h-h," and Cal coughed to an even noisier stop.

When Jonas had arrived at the rapidly filling church, he hadn't seen Steven Argyle anywhere, so after waiting a few moments he was glad to spot Simpson sitting alone and offering to make room for him. As he sat down, Jonas contrived to greet the big man with both a handshake and grasp of the right arm, as Simpson had once done to him. He was glad to feel nothing unusual, no bump near the elbow. Simpson's arm, in fact, felt larger with jovial fat than muscle. As a local informant, Simpson turned out to be a mixed blessing, however. Jonas soon discovered that he could collect quite enough curious attention on his own, just for being a stranger and somehow the rumored cause of this sad event, without the addition of Cal's garrulous whispering.

So Jonas just nodded and tried to forget his private angers and headaches, tried to concentrate on the singing and the church decorations, which Louise Telford must have chosen, and probably paid for. There were late-coloring leaves and dry stalks of corn and rusty gold chrysanthemums that reminded him of football games.

Of course. That's what the hymn was, and why it sounded like something from his childhood. It was a hymn of the season, of Thanksgiving.

> *For the beauty of each hour*
> *Of the day and of the night,*
> *Hill and vale, and tree and flower,*
> *Sun and moon, and stars of light.*

It was raining and cold outside, but for a moment the choir filled the church with sunshine. Jonas noticed that Louise Telford both smiled at the flowers and touched her nose with a handkerchief while she listened. She sat across the aisle and several rows forward of him, in a pew that had been held for her, as had the singing of the hymn which began services, too, until her arrival just a few moments ago. With her were Marjorie Dunfield, looking tautly composed, and the elderly maid named Clara who was already slumping and starting to sniffle again. But Louise sat very straight and she too brightened the church, for this was a memorial service, not a funeral, and Louise Telford wore red.

For some reason, Jonas had noticed, people who lived in rainy gray climates often seemed to dress that way. In the winter on his own island women seldom wore anything brighter than forest green or walnut brown or faded blue jeans blue, as though they were in hibernation and not allowed to blossom until summertime. Jonas was glad to see that Louise Telford didn't subscribe to the gloomy custom. Not only was her coat bright red but so was her tiny hat, and when she walked up the aisle, looking neither to right nor left, Jonas caught glimpses of shiny leather boots, sparkling jewelry, a powder blue scarf. If others didn't approve, then the hell with them, she might be saying, and it relieved Jonas to see Louise looking so positive today, so firmly in control of herself. The last two times he had seen her, the other evening when he brought Marjorie Dunfield up from Portland and then yesterday afternoon at the house, Louise had seemed fragile and confused, and it worried him.

It had begun that evening when Jonas gave her his quick report on Julie Mapes, while the maid was settling Marjorie Dunfield in a guest room upstairs. Jonas made the report flat and brief, but unlike his later sketchy reports to Argyle and the sheriff, he pulled no punches. The girl he saw in the campground, he said, was a juvenile tramp who was probably far into drugs and a lot of other things. Louise nodded as though she had already thought of that. "Yes, of course," she said nervously, absently. "So many of them are."

Then he told her what Julie looked like. "But of course you know that already, too," he added, and immediately began to regret it. Because Louise almost winced as she hurriedly admitted that yes, she *had* seen Julie before.

"Yes, I did," she said. "But I was afraid to tell you. I was afraid to tell anyone. I didn't think you'd believe me. I thought maybe it was just my eyes." She was trembling, Jonas noticed, as she explained, almost pleaded, that she had gone out in her robe before breakfast to get the newspaper from its box by the fence—an errand the gardener usually attended to—when she looked up to see someone slender and young in blue jeans staring at her from across the street. The figure was slightly indistinct in the misty dawn light, but for a startling sweet moment Louise thought it was Myron home from college, only his hair was too long, and then he ran away, only he ran like a girl, not a boy, so it couldn't have been Myron. Besides, he never would have played a trick like that—and then she remembered that Myron was a middle-aged man and he was dead, and Louise thought she was going to faint. But she managed to run into the house and call Flora Kelly, yes, that was the real reason why Louise needed help so desperately that day from someone sensible and discreet like Jonas. And now he was still here and he was still going to help, wasn't he? He wasn't going to tell anyone what she thought she had seen, was he? He wasn't angry because she hadn't told him about it before, was he?

Marjorie Dunfield came downstairs at that moment, and for a frightening second Louise couldn't remember Marjorie's name. Then the awful thing about who had been killed in the car swept back into Louise's memory and her trembling became worse. Emily was someone very important and loyal to Myron, Louise knew that, and for a moment Jonas thought she was going to speak of Myron as though he were young again only with long hair and running like a girl. But she didn't, she suddenly, desperately concentrated on planning a little light supper for Marjorie and Jonas.

He hastily bowed out. He had already upset her too much and he knew that his staying wouldn't improve matters any. Before he left, he whispered firmly that of course he wasn't angry, of course he wasn't going to tell anyone, and of course he was still going to help. He was sure that she heard him, but he wasn't sure how deeply it registered.

Now, however, when Louise glanced back through the choir's singing and noticed Jonas for the first time since entering the church, she gave him a tiny confident smile, and he knew that she was herself again. She no longer seemed uncertain and afraid. Then she glanced past him and saw someone else coming in from outside, someone whom she'd obviously been expecting, for she nudged Clara to move over and make room.

It was a younger woman who came hurrying up the aisle, intentionally making noise with her keys as she tucked them into her purse, just so people would know she'd had difficulty finding a parking place and wasn't really late to the service. She was a sleek-looking blond woman, from her sleek soft boots to her mink-trimmed suit and the transparent raincoat she discreetly shook out as she twisted to slip into the pew. Sleek were her hips as she twisted, too. She sat down next to Louise Telford and removed her hat momentarily to give her hair a little shake. She whispered something sharp to the maid that caused Clara to sit up straighter and stop sniffling. Then the newcomer looked slowly, coolly around the church, perhaps counting the house or checking to see who was missing, and Jonas finally got a good look past her blond hair to her coldly beautiful face. He nudged Cal Simpson. Who was she?

"Adele," Simpson grunted, clearing his raspy throat again, leaning closer. "Adele Frame." He jabbed a thumb toward the chairs behind the pulpit, toward the man in the dark suit who hadn't once looked up, who still just stared at the notes in his lap. "She's Chris's wife," Cal whispered, with an unexplained chuckle.

Jonas looked at her again, but he was already sure: Adele Frame was also the blond woman he had noticed through the window outside Mary's Seafood the other night, the "date" in the big car who had honked her horn impatiently for Pete, the Filipino houseboy.

> For each perfect gift of Thine
>   To our race so freely given,
> Graces human and divine,
>   Flowers of earth and buds of heaven,
> Lord of all, to Thee we raise
> This our hymn of grateful praise.

The service was brief and surprisingly moving. When the pastor spoke quietly of death, the inevitability of death, Jonas was reminded of an Irish play he saw once about fishermen lost at sea. There was a lot of keening in it, and a lot of talk about mother ocean and the sureness of drowning in her arms. Only here in Sooskamack, death lived in the forest, in the crashing trees or rolling logs, in javelins of wood or flying steel. The pastor's own father had lost his life many years ago in the old sawmill at Telford, when a huge endless band saw broke loose like a wild watchspring.

"Jesus," Cal muttered into Jonas's ear. "I saw them hauling the guys away from that one, when I was a kid. It took a whole day to get the damn thing corralled so it wouldn't take off again every time anybody touched it—"

"Please, Mr. Simpson."

The woman behind them was crying and Simpson shut up.

The pastor didn't mean to dwell on the horrors of death, he said, but they were a part of life here with which Emily Stillwell was well acquainted. Without a family of her own, Emily always gave unselfishly in many different ways to the stricken families of others, many of them total strangers to her. And now she too had died in a typical logging accident, on a road she had probably driven thousands of times before; perhaps Providence had decided on that particular death for her long ago and kindly postponed it until now.

Jonas heard soft crying in several parts of the church. It wasn't just Emily they cried for, it was themselves and their own memories, and Jonas felt embarrassed for his earlier cynicism about why people were here today. But he also wished he had asked the minister, yesterday, what kind of a driver Emily was. The sheriff claimed he didn't know, he had never ridden with Emily; he just knew she never got any tickets.

Chris Frame was even more brief. He was clearly unused to public speaking, and at first Jonas thought his strange intensity was just awkwardness. He didn't once glance toward his wife or Louise, for instance, as though to do so would rattle him. But then he spoke warmly of the past and Jonas noticed a quickening of interest among his listeners. When Frame referred to Emily's first years here as the last great years of Telford Timber, those glorious years of the new chain saws and highline logging and roaring mills, there were murmurs of agreement throughout the church. Violence and danger were still better than rotting logs and hungry kids. There were plenty of new ways to make logging safer, but not unless trees were cut and roads improved, not unless the mills were kept running.

It startled Jonas to feel frustration and resentment in the church, almost the same hidden anger he had sensed in the Fish Trap, downtown. "You just waste your time if you try to understand those woodpeckers," Charlie Tlulagit had said in the safety of the island. "They're all still woodsies, even in helicopters and hard hats, as close as ticks and leeches. But the gods planted trees just for them to cut down—and anybody who gets in their way better look out for splinters!" Only whose way did Jonas get in last night, he wondered?

There was a lot he didn't know yet. But there was no doubt about the target of Chris Frame's remarks. Nearly everyone in the church was glancing covertly toward Louise Telford. She sat stiffly and her face was pale; her eyes seemed lost in rearranging the lilies in a stained glass window. Perhaps she didn't even hear what Frame was saying; but she was the object of bitterness and anger whether she knew it or not, whether she deserved it or not, and the old lady looked more vulnerable and alone than ever. It was a relief to Jonas when Chris Frame got back on the subject of Emily, where he belonged.

His final remarks ran rapidly downhill. He and the rest of the family owed a great debt to Emily, he said, for the faithful care and service she had given over the years to his cousin, Myron Telford. Myron wasn't always in the best of health, but Emily never once complained about extra work. When Myron had problems, Emily cheerfully took care of them, even if they were unpleasant.

Frame used all the wrong words. Maybe it embarrassed him to speak of his useless cousin, or maybe he just couldn't think of anything right to say. But at least he had finally succeeded in attracting his aunt's attention. She shot him a withering glance, Jonas noticed, that might have sent a lesser man straight through the floor to damnation.

Frame must have noticed it too, for he abruptly, awkwardly sat down.

> *Now the laborer's task is o'er;*
> *Now the battle day is past;*
> *Now upon the farther shore*
> *Lands the voyager at last.*

Emily Stillwell was officially dead, and the choir was singing a last hymn to her memory, when Julie Mapes slipped silently into the church.

ELEVEN

JONAS SAW JULIE'S entrance quite by accident, as he was turning to hand a fallen mitten to the woman behind him. He almost didn't recognize the girl at first, for she wore a simple skirt and sweater beneath the slicker she shook off. She looked scrubbed and fresh, and when she removed her yellow rain hat her vivid chestnut hair fell softly to her shoulders in curls instead of strings as it had in the campground. The striking color and the widow's peak were even more noticeable now. She had stepped right out of the cafeteria line, he suddenly thought, right out of one of his sketches.

A boy, a husky young man with short blond hair and a well-trimmed bushy moustache from the nineties, came through the door after her. He looked collegiate and healthily clean. They could have been two kids on their way to a football game or even a concert. The boy, who simply had to be Mert, whispered to Julie while she giggled and peered curiously around the church.

And then others noticed them. A woman gasped quite audibly and Jonas turned to see Adele Frame half-standing, staring back as though she'd seen a ghost, while beside her Louise Telford twisted in startled confusion. A singing voice, Hagenbaugh's voice, choked in mid-note and died in muffled throat-clearing. As if at a signal, Al, the deputy sheriff, jumped up from the back row to hurry toward the newcomers. The rest of the choir faltered and practically everyone turned in one direction or another to find the cause of the disturbance. When the

76

sheriff slipped through a door behind the pulpit, which obviously led outside, a buzz of whispering rose sharply.

The pastor, however, was not one to let his ship sink without a fight. He boomed "Amen!" to the hymn and lifted his arms in stern command. "Shall we rise in prayer?"

Jonas was already pushing his way toward the aisle but Al had moved faster, and when the pastor spoke in a voice that probably carried all the way to Mary's Seafood, the startled congregation shot to its feet like a massive roadblock. For a moment, Jonas caught only glimpses of the deputy sheriff quietly hustling Julie and Mert out through the door with the help of another deputy who must have been standing outside, but at least Jonas could see that the kids didn't resist, they only looked embarrassed. By the time Jonas had worked his own way outside, the two deputies were already leading Julie and her boyfriend down the long wet steps to a squad car that was parked in front of the church with its windshield wipers running.

"Why? What did we do wrong?" Mert was saying, and Julie was laughing incredulously, "Don't tell me you need tickets to go to a funeral?"

Just two innocent kids who dropped by out of idle curiosity. It was a hell of an act, thought Jonas as he started down the steps after them, and the timing of their performance had been so perfect it was almost funny. But then the sheriff came striding into view from around the church and Jonas stopped moving. Hagenbaugh was angling toward his own car parked across the street, calling, "All right, boys. Let's go."

Jonas could easily have caught up with the sheriff and joined him, but he didn't. He stood watching while Julie and Mert were put into the back seat of the squad car and they all drove off together. The whole thing took no more than a minute. The deputies' work was so smooth it almost could have been practiced. But in their haste, Jonas realized, they had probably made a mistake.

"Where are they going? What are they doing to her?"

Jonas turned to see Louise coming out of the church. She was clinging to Adele Frame's arm and she looked frightened and confused again. For an angry second Jonas wished he had wrung Julie Mapes's conniving little neck when he had the chance.

"It's all right, Mrs. Telford," he said quickly. "I'm sure the sheriff knows what he's doing."

"I doubt it," the sleek blonde said. "He was worse than I was, in there. Oh, I'm so sorry, Louise dear." She giggled embarrassedly. "It just startled me so, that's all. Wasn't I awful?" She reached her free hand out. "You're Jonas Duncan, aren't you. I'm Adele Frame."

It was a warm, curious hand that didn't match her calculating eyes, Jonas noticed. But then her husband, Chris, came out of the church and he looked shaken.

"My God, that girl really *does* look like him!"

"Like Myron? Don't be ridiculous, dear," said Adele, still smiling at Jonas.

"Then what the hell did you scream for? Right out in church like that!"

"I did not! Chris, really, there are people," she whispered. A man was holding the door open and a few of the first women outside looked around for the missing intruders, but most people still didn't seem to know what had happened.

"It just startled me so, that's all," Adele repeated to Jonas. "Really, the girl's eyes are much too far apart."

Jonas sidestepped her and leaned close to Louise, who was still staring off down the street. "I'll talk to the sheriff," he said. "I'll talk to the girl. I'll come up to your house as soon as I can."

"No," Adele interrupted firmly. "No, we're going to Seattle," She patted Louise's hand. "First, we're going to drop Clara off at the house, remember, dear? And then we're going to Sea-Tac to put Mrs. Dunfield on her plane back to Denver."

"Of course I remember," Louise said stiffly, pulling her hand loose and turning to Marjorie Dunfield as the latter came up beside them.

"That's why we had a twelve o'clock service," Adele said to Jonas. "Mrs. Dunfield's plane leaves at four." Adele's loaded smile swiveled toward her husband. "By four-thirty, Louise and I will be buying our way through the designers' section at Frederick-Nelson. And then dinner and the Repertory, unless you forgot to make our reservations, darling."

"I always stay at the Olympic Hotel," Louise tucked in hastily, in the direction of Jonas, but then she was surrounded again by condolences for Emily.

"Look at the poor thing," Adele whispered. "Can't you see how *old* she looks? She just has to get out of here. First Emily Stillwell and now that ridiculous girl—maybe I'll persuade her to stay in town for some Christmas shopping tomorrow afternoon."

"Excuse me," said Jonas, reaching to touch Louise Telford's arm. "I heard you," he told her. "I'll call you, I'll keep in touch."

He turned and ran down the steps. He was sure now that the sheriff and his deputies had made a mistake, and he knew someone would be back in a hurry to correct it. But then Chris Frame came running after him on the sidewalk.

"Duncan, wait. I want to talk to you."

"Later, Mr. Frame. I'm on my way to the sheriff's office."

But the tall, rawboned Frame already had hold of his arm with steel fingers. "I don't know what you and Argyle think you've been up to, not telling anybody about that girl—"

"Look, I'm in a hurry—"

"We only just learned about it. Adele finally got it out of Clara on the phone this morning, what you're doing here, or part of it. A damn small part, probably."

"All right, so Clara's a snoop."

"Never mind. I just want you to know, I am Louise's closest relative, I am responsible for her. So whatever the sheriff learns about that girl—"

"I'm sure he'll tell you, Mr. Frame," Jonas said sharply. "I'm sure you've already asked him to."

Frame let go of Jonas's arm, flushing slightly. "We did speak for a moment just before the services, yes. But that's all. I was out early this morning looking at some timber and then I couldn't reach him in his office. Anyway, this is private between you and me, Duncan: The moment you find out what that brat kid's price is, let me know, understand? For Louise's sake, we've got to get rid of her quickly, and for good. So whatever she wants that's reasonable, you just let me know. I'll write a check."

Jonas hesitated, but he nodded. "I'll talk to you later," he said, and walked quickly off. Everybody wanted to get in the act. First the sheriff and now Chris Frame; soon it could be the whole First Methodist Church. But there was no time to worry about that now. Because it was the Dodge van that Hagenbaugh and his men had momentarily forgotten, or neglected in their hurry, and Jonas had spotted it from the church steps. It was parked in a vacant lot in the next block downhill.

When he got there, he found that the back door of the van was locked, but neither of the front doors was. It didn't surprise him. In this rural area probably most people still left their cars unlocked. To do otherwise was to suggest you might be hiding something, and obviously Julie and her boyfriend had nothing to hide. Oh, no, not those two innocent kids—and clean ones, too, and tidy. The whole van looked as though it had been scrubbed inside and out. There wasn't a trace of tobacco or pot or liquor, not a single condom or roach clip in dash compartment or luggage. Every sock in their rucksacks had been washed, every dish in the cupboard was clean. Even their sleeping bags must have been fumigated and fluffed in a laundromat.

Jonas searched rapidly, thoroughly, and by the time he heard the brief siren note of a returning sheriff's car winding its way through the church-crowded street, he was quite sure there was nothing to be found there. Whatever personal items Julie or Mert owned were either on their persons or, more likely hidden somewhere else for safekeeping. Jonas turned quickly to the last cupboard, which contained shaving soap, deodorant, razor blades, a washcloth. There was a cheap hairbrush on the top shelf. It was one of the things he had been looking for, and he shoved it hurriedly out of sight in his pocket as he turned to leave the van.

But in stepping over the cheaper half-rolled sleeping bag Jonas recognized as Julie's, his foot struck something lumpy and solid. He dropped to his knees. The siren was sounding again, quite close, while he pulled the zipper of the sleeping bag until he could reach far down into the bottom of it. There his fingers touched something that felt like a tightly packed cloth sack. Its material was worn and slick, as though coated with grime or dried perspiration. Attached to the hidden bundle there was a gob of loose string that had got caught in the zipper, or maybe Julie had pinned or tied it there in the hope that her secret cache wouldn't be discovered among the lumpy folds of the bag. A harder tug freed the strange object and Jonas pulled it out into the open.

It was a Raggedy Ann doll.

TWELVE

JULIE MAPES SAT sideways on a desk in the sheriff's office with her knees held tightly together, brushing her skirt down now and then, trying unsuccessfully to keep them hidden. They were bumpy and scarred and bruised, Jonas noticed, a child's knees.

Julie felt easier sitting on top of the desk than in the straight-backed low chair she'd sat in first, while she answered the deputy's slow methodical questions, while the rain washed the windows and a sluggish November fly bumped against a calendar with palm trees on it and the deputy wrote her answers even more slowly than he talked. Occasional laughter came from the next room where the other deputy named Al was asking Mert questions, but the erect little sheriff with the fancy hat never once smiled as he walked back and forth like an enemy toy soldier, listening to one interview, then the other.

They were polite to her, just the way Mert said they would be, and after she got over her first nervousness the only one who really bothered her was the tall sandy-haired man from the campground who came in late, after they went back to get the van. That's when she'd asked if she could sit on the nearby desk instead of the chair in front of the deputy, and he'd said sure, baby, even though it wouldn't give him as good a view of her legs, which really weren't bad if you liked them a little skinny. But when Jonas Duncan walked in, her heart skipped a beat and she just had to move quickly. The chair was so low she felt suddenly surrounded and aware of how her knees stuck up and how the new skirt she wasn't used to wearing kept sliding back. For a moment it was even hard to breathe.

So she sat on the desk, which was better, though she didn't risk actually looking at Jonas. Through her lowered eyelashes, however, she could see that he wasn't quite as tall as Mert but he had a skinnier bottom and his nose and chin were bigger. His voice was even deeper than she remembered from that awful nightmare in the campground, as he spoke softly to the deputy and then just leaned against the wall and listened and watched her with quiet eyes. When she straightened her skirt over her knees the first time he even smiled, and she was hopefully reminded of an actor she used to like in old westerns on TV in a juvenile home. For that brief moment of Jonas's smile she thought maybe he wasn't mad at her anymore for pointing the gun at him. Nobody else had said anything about it, so maybe he hadn't even told anyone about the gun yet. Maybe he was different, the way he looked, and didn't tell all those lies that older people always tell about how stoned or drunk or immorally depraved you are.

But then Jonas spoke. "Sergeant, why don't you get her an ice cream cone?"

So piss on him. The deputy laughed and she pretended she didn't hear. She just stared at the rain washing the windows and held her knees tightly together and watched the fly ascending the palm tree. Jonas mercifully didn't say anything more, but of course he would if she acted like it mattered, and she knew he never once stopped looking at her. He was the same filthy sadist who had sprung on her out of the night when she was scared and spaced and cruddy and God knows what else. But what did they expect? She'd never been all alone in the woods before. She'd been so scared she discovered the next day she'd even forgotten to wear her underpants to bed. So now Jonas Duncan just stood there thinking up more juvenile jokes and probably planning how he'd tell Mert and the sheriff and everybody else about her and the gun and the goddamn bears. . . .

She caught herself smoothing her skirt again. Oh, Jesus, she hated her knees!

It was pretty easy to read the girl's mind, thought Jonas, and it would probably be even easier to bust her cool. Just one snide question had already made her blush like a kid caught cheating, and her answers to the deputy were much too mechanical and overrehearsed. As an actress she was strictly an amateur who recited punctuation and stage directions along with her lines. Some real heckling would probably make her come apart entirely.

But the fingers that hovered over her skirt were trembling, and Jonas noticed that they were short sturdy fingers that looked even more childlike than her legs. She wore a couple of rings that could have come out of a cereal box. He saw the deputy eyeing Julie's legs too, only higher up, and Jonas roughly cleared his throat to keep the jerk on whatever stupid rails he thought he was on. Christ, why *wouldn't* the girl's answers sound phony and rehearsed? The questions were nothing but simple, factual ones about her past, like the names and dates of foster parents, of which she had had several, and orphanages, of which she had escaped two. Obviously Julie must have been asked these same things a thousand times by juvenile authorities, adoption agencies, social workers, teachers, judges, cops, you name it. No one in our society is as well chronicled as its least member, the unwanted orphan. No wonder Julie rattled off her answers as mechanically as an airplane hostess giving oxygen instructions.

Only one question broke the rhythm, made her pause and be a little awkward. It was about her own last name, Mapes. Since none of the foster parents had had that name, where did Julie get it? She picked it herself, she said, and a nice judge let her keep it. It came from dusty roadside billboards in places she remembered as a small child. She had always liked the name because it reminded her of the smell of sagebrush, and Jonas recognized Mapes as the name of an old-time hotel in Reno, Nevada.

Then the deputy asked her why she had come here to Sooskamack.

Julie took a deep breath and crossed her legs. "I was just curious, that's all," she said. "I don't want anything, I just came here because I was curious. Here." She produced a much-folded newspaper clipping from her purse. "Some of my friends thought I looked like somebody, that's all."

The clipping contained a photograph of Myron Telford.

"Everybody wonders about who they might be, don't they?" she asked with casual innocence. She was eighteen now.

The deputy passed the clipping to Jonas for a look. In the photograph Myron was at least fifty. The resemblance wasn't particularly noticeable.

"Who gave you this?" Jonas suddenly asked. "Who put you up to this?"

Julie took another breath. "I don't know what he means," she said to the deputy. "I got a ride with Mert because he wanted to see about a job in Seattle, that's all. I told you, I don't want anything, I didn't do anything, I won't make any trouble." She gestured toward Jonas, still not really looking at him. "So what's the matter? Why did he tell you to arrest me?"

"He didn't, and you're not under arrest," the deputy said. "This is just routine questioning."

"But what for? We didn't even make any noise in that church! So why do you treat us like we were peddling coke or something? I mean, why all these silly questions?" Her voice was rising in righteous outrage, which of course was almost justified. There was really no excuse for the sheriff interfering, hauling them in like this.

But now she *was* acting, Jonas knew, and he walked out on the performance.

Mert was slicker. To begin with, he was five years older than he looked. He was twenty-six, had attended three years of college, he claimed, had been a male nurse, bouncer at a disco, lifeguard on a cruise ship, riding instructor at a dude ranch. Most lately he'd been a security guard at one of the gambling palaces on Lake Tahoe where his cousin was a pit boss, his cousin from whom he had borrowed the van. But Mert aspired to finer things, and an old college buddy in Seattle had mentioned that he might be able to get Mert work in a TV station there. So when this kid, Julie Mapes, offered to share gasoline expenses for a trip up north with money she'd been saving from baby-sitting for some friends of Mert's in San Francisco, then he went along with the idea.

Naturally Mert didn't agree to take her, however, until Julie showed him a couple of school IDs that proved she was already sixteen instead of almost. Oh, no, Mert wanted no trouble like *that*, hauling a kid across state lines and all, so if Julie had forged those IDs, then it sure wasn't *his* fault. And of course coming out here to Sooskamack was strictly for Julie's sake. She had showed Mert that clipping, with its photograph of a guy who didn't really look much like her, as far as Mert could see; but she also told him she had heard the name Telford before, from older kids in one of those places she lived in once, like maybe they'd heard it from somebody coming around to ask questions about Julie. So Mert couldn't blame her for being curious, even though he knew it was probably just a kooky kid obsession, an orphan like her thinking she would ever find out who she really was. Until they got here, that is. Because now today, in church—well, that was really something, you know? And the way some people around here react when they just look at Julie, that makes you think. Like even the sheriff himself, the way he messed up that song in the choir, and the blond chick who stood up and hooted—wow!

Mert babbled a lot, but his seemingly ingenuous story was simple: He was nothing but an innocent bystander helping an equally innocent girl search for her identity, so what was all the fuss?

Jonas didn't learn most of it until later, however, when he looked at Al's notes. Because when Jonas walked into the room to listen, Mert's glibness began to desert him. He glanced at Jonas more and more worriedly, until finally he interrupted himself. "Excuse me, sir—is that Mr. Duncan? Does he own a blue pickup?"

"Do you?" Al turned to Jonas, surprised. "I just mentioned your name a minute ago, that's all."

Jonas nodded. "A friend of mine caught him looking at the registration slip the other day. It was inside the dash compartment."

"What? What's all this?" The pacing sheriff settled abruptly in one place.

"A friend? Hey, man, I'm sorry." Mert looked shaken. He really did look sorry. "Sheriff, I didn't know. Honest. This guy just grabbed me from behind—"

"So what did you hit him with?" The sheriff interrupted sharply.

"Nothing, sir! I just gave him a backhand jab, and then I saw he was an Indian. Christ, *I* didn't know what he might be up to, laying his hooks on me like that—"

"Oh, an Indian," Hagenbaugh said, disappointed. His glance to Jonas clearly said come on, help me nail this creep for something. The sheriff was skating on thin ice, picking Mert and Julie up like a pair of vagrants, hassling them and searching their van almost as though they were hippies from another era. He had treated them gently so far but obviously what he wanted was one good excuse not to. "How badly hurt was your friend, Duncan? Think he'd like to prefer charges?"

"I don't know," Jonas said, and suddenly stepped close to Mert, who flinched nervously when Jonas took firm hold of his right arm, apparently to demonstrate. "See, Charlie only grabbed him like this, or maybe it was higher up—" Jonas shifted his grip, taking his time. The arm was big with a weight lifter's showy muscles, but there was no lump on the bone near the elbow.

Inside the elbow, however, he felt a heavy throb. One of his fingers seemed to be resting on an artery about the size of a garden hose, and Jonas was startled to notice how long he had to wait for the next heartbeat. He kept his hand there while Mert pleaded for understanding, his voice trembling, his whole body seeming to shake. "Listen, I really am sorry! I only wanted to get your name, sir. It was your turkeys I wanted to find out about, I thought maybe you'd sell me one—"

"Turkeys!" the sheriff snorted incredulously.

"It's true! Please, Mr. Duncan. Tell your friend I'm sorry, I really *like* Indians—"

But Jonas disgustedly let go of Mert's arm. The heartbeat was unvarying, as slow and steady as a long distance runner's. Mert's nervous shaking was probably from laughter inside.

Jonas strode out the side door, into Hagenbaugh's garage. No matter how many lies Mert told, this was no time or place to go after him, or after Julie either, not without ammunition. By jumping the gun like this, Hagenbaugh had practically fixed it so no one else could even question the kids, at least not until their stories were checked. Now Mert and Julie were the harassed ones, the persecuted ones, the innocents who could get all the curiosity and sympathy they wanted in Sooskamack.

"What's the matter, don't you like somebody else doing your work for you?" Sheriff Hagenbaugh stepped out into the garage to find Jonas kicking at the souvenir remnants of Marjorie Dunfield's automobile.

"You've got enough cooks in there," said Jonas. "Why spoil your fun?"

The sheriff eyed him sharply. "This is my county, Duncan. I like to keep it peaceful. The minute you told me about that pair yesterday, I knew they might try something to get people upset, so I had the boys keep an eye out, that's all. It's too bad those kids are so clean on the surface, but whatever they're up to maybe I've put a monkey wrench in it. What the hell, if more than one person knows anything in a town this size it's not a secret anymore, anyway. At least now if they make trouble for anybody I can lower the boom. I've already got them on the record, true or false."

Hagenbaugh, Jonas was thinking, that doesn't make sense and you know it. But then the sheriff startled him by producing a soggy wallet from his pocket—Jonas's wallet.

"Where'd you get that?" Jonas gestured toward the office. "Not from them!"

"I just wish I had," said the sheriff. "But the youngster who brought it in this morning said he found it in those woods down by the Sooska River Motel. That's where you're staying, isn't it?"

Jonas glanced through the wallet and discovered that his credit cards were still there. "Huh. Nothing missing but about forty bucks."

"The youngster didn't take it. I know him from Sunday School. Only how'd you lose it? Why in hell didn't you say something?"

"I was mugged last night."

"Mugged!" The sheriff stared at him.

"A little after eleven o'clock. There was a guy in my room, it was dark, I couldn't see him."

"Well, it could have been Mert, couldn't it? Look, I can book the bastard on suspicion—"

"No. It wasn't Mert, I know that much."

"Hagenbaugh!" The shout came from outside the open garage doors, along with a squeal of brakes. Jonas hadn't realized that the brakes of a Rolls could squeal.

"Homer, what the hell do you think you're doing?" Steven Argyle said as they moved out to join him. "For Christ's sake, turn that girl loose. Turn both of them loose!"

The little sheriff seemed startled by the lawyer's anger. "Pretty quick," he murmured stiffly. "We'll be finished with them pretty quick."

"Right now," Argyle snapped. "Do you want me to wrap Judge Blair around your neck? You've got absolutely no business—"

"Damned if you don't sound like the ACLU!" the sheriff snapped back. "What the hell, Steve? Don't you realize you'll soon have a nice typed record of all the little lies they've been telling us? Names, dates, places, all in triplicate—"

"So what do you want for that, a medal? Jesus, if you think this is how to make points with Louise Telford—"

"The hell with points," Hagenbaugh barked. "The hell with old ladies, too. I didn't do it for her or you or anybody else. I'm just trying to keep the peace around here." He stalked back through the garage to his office.

"Nosy, useless bastard," Argyle stormed. "Why aren't they booked already, locked up for good, by now? Christ, the least he could have done was frame them with drugs—" He paused as he noticed the curiosity in Jonas's eyes. "Well, you don't think charging down here like a damned civil rights jackass was *my* idea, do you?"

"Louise Telford?"

"Who else? She got me on the phone just a few minutes ago, right when I was leaving for Vancouver. Told me what happened, said she didn't want anybody picked on, said I should see that the girl was released immediately, no arguments, that's it, good-bye!"

That was it, all right, thought Jonas. Now *everybody* was in the act. "I thought Mrs. Telford was on her way to Seattle," he said.

"She is now, don't you worry." Argyle sighed as he gestured to the sheriff's office. "So what's the little tramp been saying in there?"

"Nothing she doesn't want to say," Jonas answered. "Names, dates, a few of the places she remembers living in as a kid. Hagenbaugh is putting what he can out on the wire for verification; at least it's the start of a background check. And I spoke to my friend in Salem last night, he's been looking into the best agencies—"

"Skip it," said Argyle. "I already called Northwest Investigators in Seattle. My firm has used them before, they'll be the quickest."

"All right," Jonas said, feeling more and more pushed aside. Northwest was on Cy Bridgeman's list of recommendations. It was at the bottom of his list, but at least it was there.

"I tried to reach that Blue Sage outfit too, that Snow woman," Jonas said, but Argyle stopped him with a sharp gesture. The front door of the sheriff's office was opening. Mert and Julie stepped outside, paused for a moment on the sidewalk, then Julie noticed Jonas standing beside the Rolls and they turned to scamper off to the van, which was parked across the street. As they drove away, Jonas could see that Julie still looked frightened, but Mert was smiling.

Argyle stared silently after them for a long moment.

"Well?" Jonas finally said. "What do you think?"

"There might be a little resemblance," Argyle conceded.

"People see what they want to see," said Jonas. "And with all this free publicity—"

"Oh, that fucking sheriff!"

But then Argyle's eyes suddenly danced as they had when he gave Tony Pedilla the finger in the Fish Trap. "So all right, let them have their fun, it won't last long." He touched the starter of the Rolls. "I'll tell Northwest to pour on the speed, they'll get this cleaned up in a hurry. You've done what you could."

"No, I haven't," Jonas said. "Until I know what Emily Stillwell was doing here, know for sure how and why she died . . ."

Argyle didn't even hear him. Argyle was already waving, driving off.

Jonas went inside the sheriff's office and read over Al's shoulder while he typed up Mert's interview notes. Jonas got Al to call the kid who had brought in his wallet and together they searched the place in the woods where the boy had found it. There was no sign of the sketch pad, there or anywhere else in the motel area. Whoever had taken those drawings had wanted them and kept them.

THIRTEEN

THE WINCH GAVE a banshee groan as the cable tautened and bounced stiffly against the side of the road where it fell away into empty space. Jonas walked past the big truck and farther out onto the muddy shoulder, the cold canyon wind from below sticking needles of ice through his jeans. A hundred feet down the broken slope, the tightening cable stirred one end of a log that was lodged awkwardly against rocks and a stunted pine tree. There were a couple of other logs scattered like lost matches much farther down, where scraggly treetops disappeared beneath blowing cloud fragments. Somewhere still lower in the mist was the Sooska River, escaping from the cold mountains. This was where it happened, this was where Emily had died.

"Hold it!" Cal Simpson's bullhorn voice sounded small in the wind but the winch whined obediently to a stop, the cable held taut and vibrating. Another man down below with Simpson poked gingerly at one end of the log with the point of a peavey—he might as well have been trying to fend off a freighter with a boat hook—but the log moved slightly; it was apparently a few inches clear of the ground. Satisfied, the man scrambled hastily back, but Simpson noticed Jonas up above and paused to yell and wave wildly at him before joining the man in flight to one side. Jonas was already moving farther away. He had heard quite enough stories about what can happen when a cable breaks or slips loose from its load. Simpson shouted again, the winch went back to its groaning, and the last of the recoverable logs from the accident started inching upward.

According to the sheriff's report and photographs, the place where Jonas now stood was about where Johansen, coming downhill and around a corner, tried to veer out onto the shoulder in a desperate attempt to escape Emily's oncoming sedan. The dirt shoulder was wider there for a short distance and there might have been useful tracks once but now they'd been trampled by elephants. Johansen's truck had overturned and gouged out a huge ditch as it rolled and skidded to a stop thirty or forty feet down the slope, while its load catapulted in all directions. After that came the ambulance and sheriff's cars, then a couple of days later the two heavy tow trucks that it took to right and recover the cab and rear sections of the truck, not to mention the small pieces of the passenger car from lower down. And now, today, a heavy loader and truck had chewed up the whole area again as they maneuvered to hoist the logs that were close enough to reach from the road. Cal Simpson had told Jonas in church that the work would be going on this afternoon, so after Jonas finished with Al he drove his pickup out the old county road for his postponed look at the place. It was a muddy mess and Jonas was glad he'd changed into his boots and jeans, but he wished he had his long underwear on, too. The thousand or so extra feet of elevation moved winter a lot closer.

There really wasn't much to see, however. The road was seldom used anymore, not since the area it once served had been logged over so thoroughly. Its surface was a mixture of potholes and cracked narrow blacktop and stretches of loose gravel, with shoulders that varied from gutters of mud to tangles of weeds and ferns over uncertain support. There was just enough grade to require second gear in places, going downhill, but it was never steep enough so that a truck with good brakes and plenty of traction couldn't barrel at times. Coming uphill in high gear would be no sweat for an American car with a V-8 engine, though patches of mud and wet leaves made the road slippery, particularly in those places where it dipped or turned too sharply. Even a person who had driven the road a thousand times might well treat it with nervous caution if she were behind the unaccustomed wheel of an oversized, underweight sedan. The accident could easily have happened in the exact way the truck driver said. At the moment it was a lot harder to imagine it happening any other way.

Jonas saw Cal Simpson looking up again and he waved to him, then slid down through loose rocks and torn vegetation to a point where Simpson could join him.

"Hey, I didn't mean to shout at you like that, Mr. Duncan," Cal said. "But some of that wire's a little rusty. I've seen a man cut in two when a cable lets fly."

"Sure," Jonas said. "But I thought these weren't Telford logs that Johansen was carrying. Only a couple of them were, you said."

"Three. The rest belong to the Swede himself, him and his sister. It's about all that's left of a peanut tree lot they used to own, up in the hills next to some Telford land."

"So how come you take the time and trouble to rescue their logs?"

Simpson shrugged. "The Swede's leg is still banged up, and I had to come out for our own sticks, anyway, before some bastard tried to walk off with them. My Tarheel buddy over there is one of the best buckers around, and Chris Frame loaned me the truck and loader. Johansen could never raise that kind of muscle." A grin burst out as he nodded toward the log that now stood on end in its tug of war with the winch above. "Besides, we made a little deal: That one right there, that's for me. It's all mine."

"Just one log?"

Simpson chortled. "My friend, that's western red cedar. Ain't you bought any shingles lately? That's close to two thousand bucks, just the way she is, on the hoof!"

Jonas was impressed by more than the price. "Sounds like you took Johansen for a sucker," he said.

Simpson leaned over his belly to spit. "Not really. I had him by the balls."

"How so?"

Simpson eyed Jonas more warily, but then sighed. "Look. A couple days after the accident, Johansen came asking for help, that's all. Said maybe he'd cut down a couple of Telford trees, just purely by mistake, up there in the hills next to Mrs. T's property. He was scared she'd hear about it and get the wrong idea. I don't blame him, the papers were already saying it was a Telford truck in the accident, just because he'd done hauling for us in the past."

"How could she hear unless you told her?"

Simpson gestured. "There was a couple of Douglas fir logs here. The Swedes ain't got any Douglas fir that size left on their property; quite a few people might know that."

Jonas nodded. "So what you mean is, Johansen is a poacher. A thief."

"Now, don't get the wrong idea. He's no real log rustler, not like some guys these days. Why, I know a chopper pilot paid for his whole plane in two years, just snaking fallen trees out of the national parks."

"Sure, and I know guys on the island with boats who do a lot of towing at night after a big storm scatters the log booms," said Jonas. "But that doesn't clean up Johansen."

Simpson backed some more water. "So maybe it really *was* a mistake. There's no fences out there where the logs came from. It's sure nothing to go worrying Mrs. T about—or the sheriff, either!" But then he laughed and shook his head. "Oh, crap, what I mean is, the bank owns that poor bastard's truck, his creditors grab every paycheck. The Swede lives with his sister, she's a permanent cripple, she even has to have private nurses. So I won't really make him pay me that money, just for hauling his sticks to market. Jesus, everybody makes mistakes, now and then!"

"That's a fact," said Jonas, starting to move on down the slope toward a distant wheel and axle that marked the place where the car had ended up.

Simpson glanced back toward the cedar log hitching its way up toward the road, then scrambled down after Jonas. "So what the hell difference does it make to you, Mr. Duncan?"

"Oh, for Christ's sake, Cal," Jonas said with a laugh. "I'm just curious, that's all."

"Yeah," Simpson said relievedly. After a moment he added softly, "I guess I don't blame you."

They moved past a clump of windblown evergreens and down another steeper slope where the moss was slippery over big rocks, and then the ground leveled out a bit and there was no more wind. The wheel and axle had been caught between boulders. For the next hundred feet there were patches of broken glass, a headlight, a door that had been torn loose—then finally the twisted, burned hulk of the car, along with other loose pieces that were too unimportant or heavy to drag up the long slope. It was a clump of stubborn aspen that finally stopped the avalanche, and rusting metal was already blanketed with soggy dead leaves. One last vindictive log had gouged the shallow earth and rolled on to rest against a row of dwarf pines, another hundred feet farther down, and that was the end of it.

"Aren't you going to haul that one out, too?" Jonas asked.

"How?" said Simpson. "You can't even get a helicopter down this far, not even in the summer, the crazy drafts there are in a canyon like this." He shook his head. "Win a few, lose a few. That's one of our Douglas firs, too. But a couple of the Swede's logs are in the same boat—the hemlock we just passed that's stuck in those rocks and another broken one over in the next gully. I put notices on all of them, though, even his."

"Notices?"

" 'Property of Telford Timber,' and we branded them, too. There's always some nut thinks he can get away with part of a stick, but not from us, not around here. Everybody knows Chris Frame would prosecute his own mother."

Jonas nodded absently. It was the wreck he cared about, not logs. But he soon discovered that the sheriff had done a thorough job of collecting the only car parts worth looking at. Jonas couldn't find a single new dent or evidence of paint that meant anything.

"Why paint?" Cal asked.

"Because when I went to look at Johansen's truck this morning in Mount Vernon, the only parts I cared about had already been hammered or welded. I just wanted to see which vehicle hit the other one where, that's all."

"Oh. What's Johansen say?"

"I would have tried to bring him up here to show me, but apparently he got tired of talking to people and took off someplace. Al couldn't locate him for me."

Jonas walked slowly over the whole area but he soon realized he was just wasting his time. There was no more to see down here than there was up on the road. Maybe trying to take the accident apart and fit it together differently was all a waste of time. Maybe people were easier. He turned to Cal, who was blowing his nose and shivering.

"If he didn't steal those three logs, why was he so willing to give you the cedar?" Jonas asked.

"Oh, hell, I don't know." Simpson seemed sorry he'd mentioned the subject in the first place.

"Or did Johansen maybe steal that whole load? What if *all* those logs came from Telford land?"

"No, no, that's nutty. He even told me he stopped by at our old shingle mill in Telford that day to get some diesel oil. Would he do that if he had a whole load of our stolen sticks aboard? Shit's sake, Johansen's no criminal." Simpson spat for emphasis but his heavy lips were blue and he made a mess of it. He unhappily wiped his face with the back of a hairy hand.

"But you've thought about that, haven't you," Jonas said quietly. "You've asked yourself the same question, maybe wished you'd asked him."

Simpson's watery eyes glanced quickly at Jonas and then away. "Listen," he finally decided. "If that damn Swede took off someplace, I'll bet I know where. And it's easy to call and check, if you like."

"Let's go." Jonas turned to start climbing back uphill.

"His sister, she's half deaf, there's no point trying to talk to her on CB. But we can use a phone up in Telford, it's only a few more miles."

It was closer to ten miles but it didn't take long to get there, for Simpson drove almost as fast as Hagenbaugh. Jonas, following Cal's muddy Lincoln, only lagged behind a couple of times, and when he did it wasn't hard to catch up. The grade never did amount to much, and there were more and more slippery places where Jonas's pickup still had better traction than the passenger car, even without his usual load of firewood in the back. There wasn't much to slow down for, anyway. Jonas noticed an overgrown orchard through the trees on the right side, the side opposite from the river, then a rusty mailbox where a one-lane road burst out of the woods. That must have been the farm where the TV repairman had fixed an aerial, and the next corner was a blind tight one, just as the TV man had described in his statement, so that was where his near miss occurred. A couple of miles farther along there was another farm closer to the road, just a weathered old barn and house—the Jamison place—and there was the side road out of which the school bus must have come, to stop and deliver the Jamison girl before turning east, or uphill. But there was nothing to pause for there, either. It was all in the report.

So far, Jonas noticed, they hadn't passed a single car going in either direction. It wasn't until they approached Telford itself, another three miles farther along, that there were any real signs of habitation, and those were scattered and meager, a motorcycle parked beside a tilting house trailer, a dog yapping at a tethered goat, a wisp of smoke coming from a single chimney in a row of weathered shacks that must have once been well-tended company houses. There was a grocery store with a gas pump beside it and more dogs and junk cars in weed-filled yards, but there were hardly any people and most of the usable lumber had been stripped from houses and buildings, so that Telford looked like nothing so much as a ghost mining town that had been cannibalized by souvenir-hunters.

The old shingle mill, on the far side of town, was a bombed-out litter of empty sheds and sawdust piles. There was a padlock on a sagging gate in an endless high fence, which Simpson unlocked, and they drove into a yard where a couple of log trucks were parked near a diesel pump. Some of Chris Frame's men and a few independent haulers like Johansen used this place occasionally to leave their rigs or to fuel up, but there was no one in sight now. Simpson unlocked a door and they went into a barnlike room that must have once been filled with the desks of a bustling office, but now there were only dusty old newspapers and mouse droppings. Beyond was a smaller room that still contained a couple of tables and a broken couch and some chairs. There was a pile of split wood beside a Franklin stove, but the stove was cold. The whole echoing, creaking building seemed even chillier than the dying day outside.

"Was this where Myron Telford's office was?"

"No, no, that's upstairs," Simpson said, reaching for a directory that was tied to a telephone cord on one of the tables. "He had it all fixed up fancy, big hi-fi and everything. Oh, Jesus, the parties he used to throw up there." Simpson's bulbous face brightened with happy memory. "A bunch of us got to stomping so hard one night to some of his crazy music we broke a hole through the ceiling, right about here." He pawed through the phone book. "Turn on that light, will you? I can't see her damn number."

Jonas snapped a switch on the wall.

Simpson chortled. "And you know what the music was? The Beatles! Can you imagine? A bunch of crazy loggers doing an old-time stomp to Beatles records? But that was Myron for you."

"Maybe I'll go upstairs and take a look while you call," Jonas said.

"Oh, it's mostly cleaned out, now. Anyway, I haven't got a key anymore. I gave mine to Chris Frame after Myron died, so they could go through everything and make a list for Mrs. T. What was left, that is. Like there used to be these beautiful supine pictures of ladies on the wall, tits like you never saw. Myron won them in Vegas once, throwing dice with a one-eyed rancher whose very own daddy stole them right out of the fanciest whorehouse in Virginia City. Only what happened when Myron died? Some son of a bitch ripped off those valuable art works before Myron was even stuck in his grave. Shee-it!"

Simpson dialed and got his number and engaged in a brief shouting match with Johansen's sister. Apparently Simpson was right in his hunch about where the Swede had gone. Too many people had been pestering him, like some damn TV man was the latest, so as usual Johansen had taken his camper up to the Hogback for some privacy last night. As usual meant he always claimed he was being pestered by somebody, and so he was always taking off in his camper, but it was really to escape his sister, Simpson explained. And the Hogback was a good guess, this time of year, since it was a good place to collect an illegal doe or two, or maybe even an honest buck. That kind of law-breaking didn't mean a man was a crook; it just made him one of the boys.

"It's only a little ways up from here, shouldn't take us more than twenty, thirty minutes," Simpson said as they turned out the lights and moved out through the big empty room with the mice in it. At the door he looked back into the gloom and shivered. "I don't come in here much, anymore," he said, softly. "The place is so goddamned empty. So goddamned quiet."

Jonas left his pickup parked outside the shingle mill, since they would have to come back this way anyway, or almost, Simpson said. Besides, the Lincoln was warmer and more comfortable. Cal produced a bottle of Southern Comfort from the dash compartment and gave it to Jonas to open.

"Keep your eye out for snow," Simpson said. "I always carry that stuff in the winter, instead of bourbon. It goes just great, poured over snow."

"I won't wait, if you don't mind," Jonas said, and took a drink of the sweet strong liquor. It wasn't five o'clock yet, but it was already getting dark as they left the last empty building of Telford behind. Jonas handed the bottle to Simpson, who took twice as long a drink, even while dodging a raccoon with his other hand. The road they were on dropped rapidly down to join a better road, which then suddenly delivered them into the startling presence of a freeway. But they ducked under it and a moment later were back in the desolate woods once more, turning off onto a narrow logging road that wound steadily upward into the darkness of mountains.

"Show you something else," Cal said. He reached into the door compartment beside him and lifted out a tape cassette.

"Myron had a thousand of these. I got just a few he left in a box in the trunk of his car. Mrs. T said it was okay to keep them."

Cal slipped the cassette onto a tape deck and switched it on with a flourish. "Class, huh? Custom recording heads, two special speakers built in back there, the works."

Loud rhythmic music surrounded them. It was new stuff that Jonas didn't recognize, but it was neither funky nor muddy with hard noise, it was real jazz. Cal turned the volume down to a pleasant level and tipped the bottle to his lips once more. The leather on the seats was soft, the big car's springs were gentle, the Comfort was sweet.

"Tell me," Jonas said. "What was that girl of his like? The woman in Telford, years ago, who got kicked out?"

"Damned if I know," Simpson said. "She'd been a singer, once, I think. Myron claimed he found her in a Cracker Jack box, 'cause she still played with toys. But he never really talked about her unless he was drunk, then sometimes she was a no-good hippy hooker, others she was a poor little bird with a broken wing. Oh, but I didn't really know her. Back in those days, I was just a timber beast scratching ticks for a living and he was old Mack's useless son. It wasn't until maybe ten years ago that Mr. Argyle says why don't I put on shoes and come back to civilization where I could help keep Myron out of trouble. That was because once when I brought Myron home from a Saturday night stomp his mother discovered I was the only guy around who could drink him under the table and still drive. Anyway, we got to be buddies, and every once in a while we'd sneak down to Nevada for the slots or Bay Meadows for the ponies—Vegas, Frisco, Reno for the chips and chippies—oh, we had some times, all right. I had a pickup just like yours that got so you could smell it a mile away, just from lugging dead fish and sour venison to make people think we'd been on hunting trips. Of course, everyone knew different, even his mother. But Myron still had to pretend, he never wanted to hurt anybody. And I always did the driving, even after he bought the Lincoln. I held down my own drinking and took his bottle away whenever I could. If he sneaked off alone I always went after him and brought him home safe like I promised I'd do."

"Old Mack's useless son," Jonas said softly.

"Horse shit," Cal muttered even more softly, blinking at the windshield.

"It seems to be a pretty general opinion. I noticed even his cousin, Chris Frame, had a hard time saying anything nice about him in church."

Simpson shrugged and snapped on the wipers. It was starting to rain again. "Frame's a little funny, sometimes. What the hell, he's got his own problems." Cal drove silently for a while, his bloodshot eyes glued to the dark bumpy road ahead. The soft music grew harder, heavier. "Listen," he said. "Just listen to those drums. Myron could do that. He'd play along with the hi-fi up in his office for hours sometimes, all alone. He'd give up his shirt and underwear too, if you needed it." The raindrops on the windshield were spreading, sticking, turning to snow. Simpson tipped up the bottle again and handed it to Jonas, who put it back in the dash.

"Frame said some other things in church, about the old days, that Mrs. Telford didn't seem too happy about."

"The logging stuff? No, no, that was for Mr. Argyle's benefit. It must have been." Cal wiped his eyes and chuckled. "I'll bet Chris didn't even notice until he stood up to make his speech that Argyle wasn't there this morning. That's a lawyer for you. Got smart and stayed home, I guess."

"Why? What's the trouble? What's that all about?"

"Oh, how Telford Timber is run, mostly. The company, or what's left of it. Cutting down on the sawmills, selling stuff abroad. There's some guys think everything should just go on forever, just the way it used to be. They think Mrs. T owes them all a living, maybe. I don't know. Ask Chris Frame. I'm no businessman, I'm a drinker. Here, listen to this trumpet."

They rode in the warm silence of music. It was pitch black outside, and inside too. There was a lot Jonas didn't know yet, and maybe it didn't make any difference. Maybe it was a waste of time trying to take everything apart and put it back together again differently. Maybe it was a waste of time coming up here to look for the Swede, too, for when they reached the crest of a ridge, the Hogback, the wind was blowing rain and snow flat across the windshield. They nearly froze every time they stopped to struggle off the one-track road and aim flashlights through whipping trees to see if a parked vehicle was Johansen's or not. But it never was, and it was getting later and later, and when they finally did find the Swede's rattletrap homemade camper, and then spent another half hour locating Johansen himself, there was nothing he could tell them anyway.

The Swede still held his rifle in one hand but he hadn't fired it. The bullet that entered one side of his head and blew out the other side had come from much farther away. His blood was black and half-frozen. His snow-salted body was stiff with rigor mortis.

FOURTEEN

THE SUDDEN GRAVEL ROAR of a chain saw split the silence. Jonas sat up with a start, sloshing drops of his coffee onto the worn rug of the doctor's sitting room, which apparently doubled as a waiting room later in the day. The doctor's wife had provided Jonas with the coffee and then left him here to wait while her husband took a shower and shaved, but apparently her coffee wasn't strong enough to compensate for Jonas's night of lost sleep.

The chain saw took care of that. It was louder than a thousand roosters, more grating than chalk on a blackboard, startling enough to jolt hibernating creatures out of their slumber for miles around. Jonas dabbed at the drops of coffee with his handkerchief and stood up to drink the rest of the cold brew while he walked to a window and peered into the unveiling dawn.

It was a neighbor who was the cause of the ungodly racket, whacking away at a pile of small logs, chopping his firewood the easy way. He looked slightly older than Jonas, and why was it that everyone who got his first driver's license in the early nineteen fifties had to make noise for the rest of his life? Was it because they were all too young for the fun and games of World War II or Korea? Too old to be cured by Vietnam? Did they miss their firecrackers? Was that why they all wanted motorcycles and oversized outboards and backfiring jalopies, only you couldn't even give one away if it had a muffler on it? And then came the snowmobiles, of course, to explode and chew up whatever peace and quiet the trail bikes had missed. In the north country, macho was a snowmobile with a rifle carried in a saddle holster, cowboy style, for the handy shooting of power line insulators and Forest Service trail signs and lonely cabin windows. That noisy neighbor could be reached with a slingshot, Jonas decided, unless someone threw boiling water or sicced a big dog on him first.

But then the saw took a breather and Jonas noticed the grandfather's clock beside him. He realized it was he and the tardy November sunrise who were out of step and behind times, not the neighbor, for it was almost eight o'clock. Jonas had been sleeping with that cup in his hand for over half an hour. The neighbor pressed the button on his sputtering saw and this time it roared even louder through a heavier log, but the sound was part of the day now and belonged there. Jonas was reminded of the tarp-covered pile of logs beside his own woodshed that awaited cutting to fireplace size. It was a task he'd been saving for a special day, along with clearing a few dead trees that might fall in the wrong direction in a storm. Of necessity, a small chain saw was one of the first things he'd bought after he moved to the island, and he had to admit there was something magical about the way it just melted through a log or tree. Even that machine-gun noise was endurable, if you made it yourself, that is. It was seductive, hypnotic, the kind of noise that drowns out thought. And then it was so easy to make one more cut, and the next one after that was even easier—unless you were trying to fell an alder and it suddenly split or caught the chain or flipped the whole saw back at you. There was a man in Whale Harbor who cut off his own leg that way. For alder, use an axe. But with a chain saw . . .

"My God, are you still squeezing that cup? I saw you were sound asleep, so I went ahead and ate breakfast. Here, warm it up." The elderly doctor poured from a coffee pot in his hand and Jonas caught the blessed scent of brandy. "I make it better than my wife does," he winked. "She'd be glad to fry you some eggs, though."

"No, thanks. I already told her, I had a big breakfast just a couple of hours ago in Seattle."

"Seattle?" The doctor was surprised. "I thought you spent last night with the sheriff, out on the Hogback."

"I did until I started to freeze to death, then I remembered an errand I had to run in the city." Jonas sipped the beautiful coffee. Taking a hairbrush to Seattle wasn't the kind of errand the doctor needed to know about. Or anyone else, for that matter, at least not until Jonas heard back from his ex-cop friend Fred, chief of security at the Snoqualmie Hotel. Fred knew a lab man at Seattle police headquarters who would do a private job on the hairbrush.

The doctor had been up all night too, doing an autopsy on the Swede. "So what do you want to know, Mr. Duncan? I gave it all to Homer on the telephone."

"Oh, just the usual. I wanted to stop by, anyway." Jonas was trying to make his visit seem as casual as possible.

The doctor obligingly rattled off a summary: Cause of death was massive hemorrhage and heart failure from a single high-velocity bullet that passed through the brain and burst Johansen's skull in egress. Death was almost instantaneous; he died where he fell. There were traces of alcohol but that would be par for the deceased and it probably wasn't enough to cause intoxication. As for time of death, that was almost impossible to pinpoint . . .

"But it usually takes eight to twelve hours for rigor mortis to set in," Jonas interrupted. "And if we found him stiff a little after seven-thirty in the evening—"

"All right, you've read a book. But it was cold up there, plus a lot of other factors. The best I can say is eight hours minimum up to fifteen or twenty hours maximum, that's the most time he could have been dead. I doubt if it happened in the middle of the night, though."

"Why?"

The doctor shrugged. "Not as many stray bullets flying around then, that's all. You ever try hunting at night?"

"It's not so hard, if your target is close enough. Or if you use a flashlight."

"Jack-lighting, sure. But a deer has a bigger eye than a man does, to reflect the light. And when you're at least sixty or eighty yards away—"

"How do you know that distance?"

"Experience, nature of the skull penetration and damage."

"You said 'high velocity,' too. But you didn't find a slug in Johansen, did you?"

"No, and none of you guys who tromped around out there found one either, Homer says."

"But still based on all that, your guess is—"

"I don't guess, Mr. Duncan," the doctor snapped, but then he laughed. "Damned if you don't sound like you've been in a courtroom once or twice. Well, so have I. About a hundred times. I'm considered rather an expert on gunshot wounds, and Lord knows I ought to be, the practice I get, around here."

Jonas smiled. "Sorry. What else?"

"The entry wound was a nice clean one. If you ever do find a slug or casing out in those weeds, I'll lay money it's from a caliber thirty."

Jonas held out his empty cup and the doctor refilled it.

"Thanks," Jonas said. "You've worked on Johansen before, haven't you?"

The doctor poured the rest of the coffee into his own cup.

"Like after his wreck, when Emily Stillwell was killed?" Jonas persisted. "I noticed your name in the record."

The doctor shrugged. "I was at the hospital when he was brought in, that's all. There wasn't much to do on him, the X rays showed no fractures, just a little sewing here and there."

"Did he talk about what happened?"

"No, no, he was never much of a talker. Maybe swore at the nurses now and then."

Jonas tried again. "I suppose a doctor in a place like this gets to know almost everybody. They all come to you for something, sooner or later."

The doctor hesitated. "Well, there are other medical men in these boondocks, you know. I'm mostly just general surgery."

"Of course. But I was thinking of something Cal Simpson told me last night. He wasn't here, he said, that day when Myron Telford died, six months ago."

"That's right. Cal was out of state running errands for Myron. The poor guy still feels guilty for leaving him alone, I guess."

"But you were the one who handled everything, he says. You not only rushed Myron to the hospital, you also had to take care of his mother."

"There wasn't much rush," the doctor said. "Myron was found dead at the bottom of the stairway. Had a brain clot the size of your thumb, all his veins were a mess, he would have had one worse stroke after another. Like I told Louise, it's just lucky he *was* alone and took that fall."

"I guess nothing could have eased her shock, though," Jonas said. "She must have loved Myron very much, even if they weren't always close. I have the impression they could just never reach each other."

The doctor gave Jonas a curious glance. "Credit old Mack for some of that," he said dryly. "But now if you'll excuse me, I have patients to see this morning."

"What's the matter, is Mrs. Telford a patient of yours?"

"At times. She is also a friend. So if it's questions about the Telfords you're trying to ask—"

"I won't step on your ethics," Jonas said. "But, doctor, you know why I'm in town. You must. Everyone seems to."

"Homer told me your credentials, and my wife was in church yesterday, if that's what you mean. But I haven't seen that damn girl, and I think it's all nonsense, anyway. She can't be Myron's daughter."

"Why not? Was Myron Telford impotent, maybe?"

"Oh, hell, no. It just doesn't make sense, that's all. Emily Stillwell thought it was impossible."

"She did? Why? What did she tell you?"

"Nothing specific. Anyway, that was years ago." The doctor paused. "Only now will you please tell me what any of this has to do with last night? Johansen's death was just a hunting accident, wasn't it? That's all Homer said."

Jonas hesitated. "Pretty convenient hunting accident. There have been some other things that bothered me."

The doctor frowned. "Maybe you don't know this country. All the gun-happy creeps in creation come out here, this time of year."

"I know."

"What other things?"

"Doctor," Jonas said quietly, "I'm just not convinced yet that Emily Stillwell's death was an accident."

The doctor finished the rest of his coffee and slowly put the cup down. "All right," he said. "What else do you want to know?"

"One medical question." Jonas touched his own arm near the elbow to demonstrate. "What is it if a man has a lateral bump across this bone, right here—pretty good size but it obviously doesn't impair his movement or strength—"

"In the bone itself? It could be several things, calcium deposits, birth malformation—"

"Johansen didn't have anything like that on his right arm, did he?"

"No, no. The only one like that I remember was nothing but a badly set fracture from childhood. It was on the arm of a man whose tractor had turned over—" The doctor stopped, watching Jonas.

"Pedilla," said Jonas, suddenly remembering. "He turned a bulldozer over once. Was it a man named Tony Pedilla?"

"I didn't tell you that," the doctor said evenly.

"All right, I didn't hear it. But now, about Louise Telford. How strong is she mentally? How much strain, anxiety—"

"I'm no psychiatrist, Mr. Duncan. I suggest you don't try to be one."

"But she did have a breakdown of some sort, didn't she? I gather there's been talk of her going away—"

"Of course. Louise took Myron's death very hard. She couldn't eat or sleep, kept blaming herself, had spells of thinking he was still alive, got so worn out and fragile she'd start crying if you looked at her cross-eyed. One of the doctors wanted to put her in a Seattle hospital, but thank gosh we talked him out of that. Because after a while she started seeing people again, my wife got her interested in gardening again, a woman over on your island phoned her all the time, that helped. Bit by bit Louise has been pulling herself out of it."

"She seems confused at times, though—forgets things—I've wondered if I was upsetting her too much, or if she's just getting a little senile, maybe."

"Damn right she is! So are you, so am I. By the time we're thirty we're all sliding downhill."

"Doctor, I'm only trying to help her. Why are you so defensive?

Has anyone else asked these questions? Has anyone ever suggested that Louise Telford might have to be declared incompetent, for instance?"

The doctor hesitated. "As in unable to handle her own money, you mean. Is that what you're driving at?"

"There's quite a bit of money to handle."

The doctor hesitated even longer. "If you ever quote me on this one, I'll kill you," he finally said. He moved to pick up the coffee cups and stack them together. "For a while, yes, that subject came up at least once or twice a week. If it wasn't to me it was to her internist. Or a call to a psychologist, over in Burlington. Or questions at the hospital library about books on geriatrics, plus the travel folders and condominium ads and loving advice about how much happier she'd be basking in some desert resort with all the other dying dodoes. Well, maybe there isn't much to keep Louise here in the woods anymore, but she's almost back on her feet, and as far as I'm concerned, she is fully competent to make her own decisions, about *everything*."

"So now along comes a girl named Julie Mapes," Jonas said softly. "To remind her of Myron, to upset her again."

"You could be pretty disturbing yourself, Mr. Duncan." The doctor gave him a long hard look. "Whatever it is you don't know yet, you'd better find out in a hurry. Before you go using the word murder out loud, you'd better be damn sure you're right."

"Who was it who asked all the questions, gave all the advice?"

"Adele Frame used to be a nurse once. I'm sure she means well, but God save us from nurses who know too much."

FIFTEEN

BY THE TIME Jonas arrived at the shingle mill in Telford, Chris Frame was already there waiting for him. Jonas didn't drive by way of the old county road this time, but took the lower, newer, shorter route that passed below Telford to join the freeway farther on.

Frame had even less distance to drive, since the mill he managed, the last of the big Telford mills, was on a closer inlet of the Sound than Sooskamack. But even so, Frame must have left his office the moment after Jonas's phone call; he must have driven very fast.

"What's it all about? Why'd you want to meet me here?" Frame asked, as he unlocked the big wooden gate.

"There's something I thought maybe you could show me, before Mrs. Telford and your wife get back from Seattle."

"All right. But what's the story on Johansen?" Frame's darting curiosity glittered close to the surface, like minnows. "Just a hunting thing, wasn't it? Some trigger-happy idiot blazing away at anything that moves?"

Jonas shrugged. "Unless there's someone around here who had reason to kill him, I suppose."

"The Swede?" Frame's laugh sounded forced, but maybe he wasn't the kind of man who laughed naturally about anything. "Duncan, that square-head could have got himself killed with a tire iron or broken bottle almost any Saturday night. But shot in cold blood? No, no. I'm sure he never had any real trouble with anyone."

"Except his creditors, maybe? He was pretty hard up for money, I gather."

"Who isn't, these days?"

"Not everybody will steal for it."

"Steal what? A few little logs, like Cal's been worrying about?" Frame snorted. "Simpson is an old nanny. He still fusses over 'our mill' and 'our logs,' as though his boozy benefactor were still around. Cal was never anything but Myron's gofer, you know. Now he just can't get it through his skull he's not needed anymore."

"I wanted to see Myron's old office, last night, but Simpson didn't have a key."

"Of course not. I took it away from him. I didn't want *him* throwing parties up there, setting the place on fire."

They walked through the yard where the log trucks were still parked, but there was no one else around. Frame paused by the diesel pump to check its meters, jiggle them, and finally kick the pump.

"Sons of bitches," he muttered, then moved on, gesturing, explaining. "The damn weirdos in those old houses out there, they sneak in with a long hose, sometimes. Twice I've had the sheriff run the whole gang out, but back they come, the beards and long dresses, vegetarians, addicts—and you know what they all say?" His voice rose in sarcastic mimicry. " 'Myron told us it was all right to live here as long as we like.' Hah!" They walked into the old building and up the dark stairway where stricken Myron had fallen to his death. Frame unlocked the door to Myron's old office.

It was a big room with comfortable leather chairs scattered around and windows looking out toward the snowy mountains. There was a walnut desk, a large file cabinet, and an ancient safe by one wall, but otherwise it was furnished more like a club room than a place of work. It was even a little warmer than the empty rooms downstairs, a fact that the usual spiders of this climate seemed to appreciate. There were several antique lamps and brass cuspidors; an ornate Victorian bar bracketed one corner.

"I've told Argyle we ought to move the rest of this stuff out of here before the creepos get it. But oh, no, he doesn't want to bother Aunt Louise with any more decisions for a while."

Jonas looked in the desk drawers, which were filled with a litter of stationery and old magazines. He turned to the safe. Its door was open and rusting.

"Nothing there, now," Frame said. "But you know what they found after Myron died? Threatening letters from gamblers about money he still owed, overdue bills from private poker clubs, stuff not even Simpson had ever heard of, from times when Myron sneaked off alone."

"Big spender, big loser."

Frame shrugged distastefully. "It wasn't just his own money he threw away, either. They've discovered that since the time Emily Stillwell retired, the only company funds Myron handled have just about disappeared. Can you imagine? All those years Aunt Louise had been keeping the company going just for her precious son, hoping he'd finally turn into something, and all he turned into was a thief, a crook."

"How much was involved?"

"Oh, that's not my department. Argyle and the bank, they're the executors, not me. And of course they've kept everything as quiet as possible, let sleeping dogs lie, mustn't frighten his mother, mustn't desecrate the name of Telford!"

Bitterness makes people smaller, thought Jonas. Chris Frame was shrinking again as he had in church.

"Mr. Argyle suggested there might be some old letters or files here that would have reference to Myron's search for a daughter. Back in the old days Emily Stillwell hired some detectives, for instance."

Frame looked dubious. "Emily closed the last of the shingle mill books before she retired and moved to Portland. She probably cleaned up most of his personal files at the same time, don't you think?" His gesture took in both desk and file cabinet. "That's mostly just junk they decided to leave here for a while, to save hauling into town, I guess, or maybe they didn't want Aunt Louise stumbling into her son's private pornography. Not that I've ever looked. It's none of my business."

Jonas was already looking in the top drawer of the cabinet. There was a pile of old hunting and fishing magazines, several dog-eared files containing travel folders, hotel brochures, airline schedules, a litter of credit card receipts and canceled checks. A big brown envelope contained ancient newspaper clippings with photographs of grinning mill workers and smoking mill stacks.

"That's how it looked around here in the old days," said Frame, leaning over his shoulder. "See there? That's five freighters all loading at once, down at the mill I manage now. We used to be one of the biggest plywood producers in the state, you know. Telford Timber had half a dozen mills, and we logged all our own land, too. Had our own railroad, our own fleet of tugs—Lord, you wouldn't have known this place!"

"What happened?"

"Well, the shingle mill closed when we ran out of cedar. But there was a big burn not long after that, so when old Mack died, the board—Aunt Louise and her lawyer friends, that is—they broke things up, sold what they could, put timber holdings out on lease. It made sense at the time, I guess." Frame shook his head regretfully. "The trouble was, I was barely out of college, there was nobody else left in the family to stop it, to even argue. Just Myron is all."

In the second drawer there were more receipts and canceled checks, but the executors had already listed these, Frame said, obviously to ward against claims. There was a folder filled with smudged carbons of badly typed letters and notes that Myron himself must have written in his last year, when even his handwriting seemed to be running downhill. "I thought the logging business started booming again," Jonas said, mostly to make Frame stop looking over his shoulder.

"Oh, it did! There were a dozen years there when the timber cut in Washington was tripled. But in that same time a third of the sawmills were shut down. Later it became half. And you know why? Because the big conglomerate-lovers like Argyle, they didn't care if ordinary people got tossed out of their jobs. The price of lumber is still sky-high, but do our local mills get any of that action? Oh, no, the Japs want wood products so bad they take the whole hairy logs and just dump them into ships for milling in Japan! That's what most of the cargoes still are, going out of Grays Harbor and Port Angeles. People scream about all those pretty trees being chopped down faster and faster—well, that's because half the Northwest has been turned into nothing but a goddamned tree farm for Japan. . . ."

He checked himself. Jonas wasn't listening; he had lowered Myron's letters to stare absently at the closed bottom drawer of the file cabinet.

"When was the last time you were in this office, Mr. Frame?"

"Four or five months ago, I guess. When they figured most of Myron's bills were in, the man from the bank made his final check and we locked her up."

"Has anyone been here since?"

"Nobody else has a key. Why? What'd you find? Is there something about that girl in one of those letters?"

"No, no," Jonas said.

"I don't believe you. You got me going on the logging stuff just so I wouldn't notice what you were doing." Frame grabbed the folder out of Jonas's hand and sat down on the other side of the desk to look through it.

Jonas shrugged and reached curiously to brush a tangled spider web from the handle of the bottom drawer. Spiders drop down from above to weave their webs—but there hadn't been a single thread on the handles of the upper drawers, Jonas had noticed, even though the web was obviously collapsed, disconnected from above. The shell of a fly was woven into it and when Jonas touched it with his fingers it didn't come apart, it was still relatively fresh.

While Frame peered suspiciously at Myron's old correspondence, Jonas opened the bottom drawer and leafed rapidly through its contents. There were *National Geographic*s, ad folders from hotel-casinos, a box of poker chips, a stack of unused tapes, cartons of shotgun shells. But he saw nothing that might relate to Julie Mapes, just as there was nothing about her in any of the letters. Nowhere was there any pornography.

Jonas shifted his chair slightly so the pale sun through the window would reflect better on the face of the cabinet. Now he could see that there was no faint film of dust on the top two drawers as there was on the bottom one. He touched the tangle of spider web again, rubbed it between his fingers. A broken web should dry out quickly, turn almost to powder, but here there were still remnants of silken substance that felt a little sticky, a little moist.

"What the hell are you doing?"

"I'm all through," Jonas said, rising abruptly. He took the folder from Frame and tossed it carelessly back into the file cabinet. "Let's go. There's nothing about the girl here, not anymore, nothing else worth looking at."

But there had been, he was thinking. There must have been something of interest or value in one of those two upper drawers—and someone had taken it out more recently than four or five months ago.

A *lot* more recently.

SIXTEEN

SKOOKUM CORNERS (Gas 'n' Ammunition) was nothing but a crossroads store at the intersection of two muddy gravel roads, but its stale doughnuts were gone by nine o'clock in the morning, and by the time Jonas got there, around noon, an entire month's supply of beer had been sold out. Not even the opening day of trout season nor the best attended of summer forest fires could compare with today's invasion, today's bonanza. Skookum Corners was only a few miles from the Hogback and therefore the best place to set up a command post, a checkpoint for the endless carloads of angry men whom the sheriff's deputies were herding out of the woods like rabbits. By now the narrow road was choked with campers and trailers and motor homes. When Jonas found Hagenbaugh, the sheriff was up to his ass in outraged deer-hunters.

Jonas tried to tell him what he had seen in Myron's office in the old shingle mill, but the tight-lipped sheriff was in no mood to listen. He had been here since shortly after dawn and so far hadn't found a single damned hunter who would even admit he had been anywhere near the higher ground of the Hogback yesterday morning, let alone seen or heard anything helpful. They were all blind or deaf or dumb. Even the ones Hagenbaugh knew personally, the handful of scattered locals whom he had questioned earlier, the ones whose campers had been parked off the Hogback road itself, were no help. Each had his own private theory about where to lie in ambush for the stray panicky deer who came fleeing the daily battle of sportsmen below. Each wanted to be left alone, and paid little attention to anyone else; not one of them would admit even to knowing that Johansen had been in the area.

"Don't spray blood on that pretty hat! One drop'll get you twenty years!" There was a burst of laughter from a group around a water trough where an old man was making a fortune dressing out deer.

"So the mighty hunters can go back to the city and say they did it themselves," muttered Hagenbaugh as they walked past and into the store. The coffee there tasted like crankcase drainings.

"Yesterday morning," Jonas said. "Why are you only looking for people who were near the Hogback yesterday morning?"

"Simple," said the sheriff. "Taking the doc's outside figures, the Swede must have died sometime between midnight the night before and noon yesterday—"

"That's right. But it could have happened in the earlier part, before dawn."

"No," said Hagenbaugh. "When I gave his sister the bad news— she lives down toward the Sound on this same road—she told me Johansen always checked in two or three times a day on CB, just to make sure she was okay."

"And he did yesterday?"

The sheriff nodded. "Eight-thirty A.M. He seemed to be getting interference but she could hear him all right, he sounded just as lively and sober as any other day, she said. So that's it. Johansen was shot sometime after eight-thirty yesterday morning and before twelve noon at the latest."

Out the window they could see Al trudging closer with an harassed look on his face.

"What about guns?" Jonas said. "A thirty caliber isn't always the best deer rifle, is it?"

"Oh, no, we've only seen about fifty of them, so far," Hagenbaugh snapped. "Duncan, some of these guys would use a cannon if they had it. Don't you know how many army surplus weapons have been sold in the past forty years? Damn it, the gun's not going to get us anywhere."

Al came in crying. There was a county supervisor on his radio who wanted to know what was going on. A state game warden was in danger of being clobbered any minute for using the opportunity to check tags and licenses. A nosy reporter had shown up and wanted a statement. Somebody was calling his congressman. So a dumb Swede caught a stray bullet, what of it, said the sportsmen, who gave a damn? How long had it been since a sheriff got lynched?

"How'd we get into this mess, anyway?" Hagenbaugh groaned. "And now you bring me spider webs and file cabinets. Duncan, who says there's a connection between any of this stuff in the first place? *Any* of it?" An impatient horn was honking somewhere. "For Christ's sake, Al, tell them to hold their water! We've stopped the road blocks, we'll be through here in a couple of hours." He put down his coffee. "Come on, I'll give that bastard his statement now."

Jonas moved after him. "What are you going to say? Just call this another accident, like you did Emily's death?"

The tiny sheriff glared at him. "What the hell else can I call it?"

He strode off with Al, and Jonas didn't follow. This was the dirty part of police work, the endless, obligatory search for evidence that almost never turned anything up. Jonas walked slowly back down the crowded road toward his pickup. If they hadn't found a witness from the Hogback so far they probably never would, and he might as well stay out of it, or at least wait a while before he heckled the sheriff with any new problems.

The sudden cannon blast of an airhorn smashed against his back. There was a chorus of hooted laughter as Jonas automatically leapt for his life—and then realized that the deafening sound only came from a chrome-decorated truck loaded with beer-drinkers, which had been creeping along the road behind him.

He did his best to laugh as he gave the driver the obligatory fuck-you gesture. No wonder Hagenbaugh was getting so damned edgy. But as Jonas watched the gaudy vehicle swish past like a fat sequined whore, he suddenly forgot the ringing in his ears and the laughter, everyone's laughter. He hurried to pile into his pickup. He worked his way quickly out of the traffic jam, and when he reached a better road he poured on the speed.

Burlington was some distance away but it was the nearest town of any size. He couldn't find exactly what he was looking for there, but what he found was close enough. He signed the rental papers and then asked where he could safely park and lock his pickup. The clerk looked at him as though he were crazy, but made no objection as Jonas drove rapidly away in their best rental car, a big American-made sedan.

When he got back to Skookum Corners, its hour of glory was about over. Jonas found Al and another deputy talking to the last of the deer-hunters while the sheriff leaned tiredly against his own car, watching the old man hosing blood and guts into a hole in the ground he'd dug for that purpose. Not that any mere covering of dirt would stop small critters from burrowing, the old man cackled, or stop larger ones from digging up these fragrant remains. Tomorrow he'd dump a load of heavy rock on top, but in the meantime he'd better just keep his dogs inside, and if he happened to get him a nice contraband cougar skin with an easy shot from his window tonight, then surely the sheriff wouldn't go telling, would he?

The sheriff wasn't even listening. "Oh, Lord," he sighed as he saw Jonas approaching. "Can't your damn spiders and file cabinet wait a while longer?"

"Not if you've got a set of pass keys, so we can take a look in Myron's office on our way back to town. Come on, I'll drive you home. You can let one of your boys take your car, can't you?"

Hagenbaugh started to object but then took a sharper look at the sedan Jonas had just climbed out of. He didn't even ask what had happened to Jonas's pickup.

"I guess so," he said.

When they reached the old shingle mill in Telford, the main gate was already unlocked, apparently by the driver of a log truck that was parked beside the diesel pump. Hagenbaugh had no trouble opening the main building with a pass key—a strictly legal entry, he pointed out, since Chris Frame was always asking the sheriff's office to keep an eye on the place. The lock on Myron's office was slightly tougher, but the sheriff knew locks and with a little tinkering got that one open, too.

Hagenbaugh had brought a small fingerprint kit from the trunk of his car, and after squinting carefully at the file cabinet he conceded that it probably had been opened recently, just as Jonas had said, so he started dusting the handles of the top two drawers.

Jonas didn't really expect that they would find any definable fingerprints, and they didn't, except for one that turned out to be his own. But Hagenbaugh agreed it was strange for two handles to be so clean when the bottom one was still grimy with moisture and dust, the usual deposit of time in this humid cold climate. So there was little doubt that the two upper drawers had not only been opened recently, but their handles and faces had been at least partially wiped by either a cloth or gloved hands.

But how recently? "Hell, that's the trouble," said the sheriff. "It could have been yesterday or last week or last month, there's no way to tell. So maybe one of the local creeps just broke in one night to snoop around, look for souvenirs or pills." Hagenbaugh rose tiredly. "I'd better check those locks again, though."

Jonas glanced out the window. A man eating a candy bar was moving toward the log truck by the diesel pump. "I've got to take a leak," Jonas suddenly decided. "I'll meet you outside."

He caught up with the man just as he was about to start the engine of his truck. Fortunately, he had noticed Jonas before, in church yesterday sitting with Cal Simpson and just a few minutes ago entering the mill with Hagenbaugh, so the man was friendly and listened to what Jonas said, and then listened with even more interest when Jonas pulled a twenty dollar bill out of his pocket. By the time the sheriff came out of the building, Jonas was already climbing in behind the wheel of his rental car, and when they drove off, the log truck was still parked beside the diesel pump.

Outside the mill, Jonas turned off the road they had come into town on and took the rutted street that led to the old county road instead. It was the slower, longer route to Sooskamack, but the sheriff made no comment. There was a muddy area near the outskirts of Telford, and Jonas touched the gas pedal lightly as they splashed through it. The rear wheels immediately spun. He pressed the brake and the car jerked toward one side.

"Any tires on this hearse?" Hagenbaugh muttered. It pleased Jonas to notice that the sheriff's legs had stiffened slightly when the brakes grabbed. Like many good drivers he probably hated to ride with anyone else.

"There's some tread left," Jonas said. They reached a more solid paved area and he stepped on the gas again, harder this time. The wheels spun almost as quickly as they had in the mud, and it took a hasty turn to stop the car from sliding sideways.

"Plenty of power," he said, slowing down.

"Too damn much," Hagenbaugh muttered. "For the weight, that is. But it's got an awful pretty dashboard. And all this fancy upholstery, and the chrome and striping out there—real Detroit class. Only look out for those brakes, for Christ's sake!"

That time the skid was unintentional. Jonas hadn't noticed the dark layer of wet leaves on the road as he slowed for a corner.

"This isn't quite the same model as Marjorie Dunfield's, you know," Hagenbaugh said. "Hers was a year earlier, had the next size engine too, I think."

"You mean hers would have skidded even easier? This was the closest I could find in Burlington." Jonas rolled his window down a little. There was no sound but the soft purr of the big car's muffler and the ever-present ticking of the windshield wipers. It wasn't raining at the moment but there were patches of mist in the hollows and big splats of water fell now and then from soggy evergreen branches overhead. They were approaching the Jamison farm and Jonas slowed almost to a stop as they passed the entrance of the side road.

"That's where the school bus came from, when it stopped to let out the Jamison kid, right? And then turned to go up toward Telford?"

"That's not what you brought me here to show me," Hagenbaugh said. "What's so all-fired important about that?"

"It's part of it," said Jonas. "Did you find anything more in Myron's office?"

The sheriff shook his head. "I don't think anybody tampered with those locks except us. Whoever was in there lately must have had a key."

Jonas nodded. "That's what I figured. And whoever opened that file cabinet probably wore gloves, but that doesn't necessarily mean it was to keep from leaving fingerprints. Of course, men usually take off their gloves when they come inside. But women, even to open their purse in a store, they often leave their gloves on."

"Sounds like you've stood in line at the bank."

Jonas leaned closer to the window to listen again. He thought he could hear another car or truck in the distance but he wasn't sure yet.

"Anyway," he continued, "a woman wearing gloves could easily have taken out whatever files or papers she wanted, particularly if she knew where to find them. And she must have, because only two drawers out of three were even touched."

Hagenbaugh shifted slightly in the wide seat but his expressionless eyes never left the road. Jonas glanced at the speedometer and increased his speed a little. He could definitely hear the rumble of a truck in the distance now.

"Emily Stillwell would have known where everything was," Jonas said. "When Mr. Frame told me who had keys he didn't mention her name, but Myron's old secretary *must* have had a key to that office."

"We never found any keys after the accident," the sheriff said after a moment. "Of course, her purse was thrown out of the car with her body—things were burned, scattered all over hell and gone, so it doesn't mean much. All those leaves and ferns, you could lose a whole hardware store down there."

"I know. I did a little looking myself."

The sound of a horn floated through the woods, loud and then soft and then louder again as the truck behind them rounded a corner. Jonas was reaching a straighter stretch now, where the road dropped more rapidly before climbing another small hill and then another after that. He automatically speeded up when the horn sounded again and the distant truck came into view in his rear vision mirror.

Hagenbaugh twisted to look back for a moment, then turned to watch the road ahead once more. "Bill Staples, I guess," he said. "That was his rig in the mill yard."

When Jonas reached the crest of the first hill he glanced in the mirror again. The big log truck was barreling down the middle of the road to hit the low spot with the most speed possible.

"Really moves, doesn't he," Jonas said.

"They're all cowboys."

"I noticed quite a few of these little uphill stretches. So I guess it would be pretty hard for a truck to really go out of control on a road like this, unless your brakes went out entirely."

Hagenbaugh grinned. "Why do you think we built it this way?"

"We?"

"Us suckers, the taxpayers. Don't you know that's how the Forest Service spends most of its money—to build logging roads? The county just put a little blacktop on this one, later on. Oh, but guys used to jackknife here once in a while. The new road's a lot faster."

As Jonas crested the second rise he could see that the truck had gained considerably on them. But then the road twisted through woods, the corners were tighter, and the sounds of the truck faded. A mile or so farther along, when they passed the mailbox and old orchard, he could hardly hear it at all. He was about to comment on how soon after reaching this road the TV repairman had nearly collided with Johansen, when a blast of the truck's horn from behind jolted him back to the present. The truck couldn't be more than half a mile away. It hadn't slowed down, the woods had only muffled its sounds for a while.

Jonas concentrated on his driving, but apparently not hard enough. He tapped the power brakes a little too firmly on a wet corner. He didn't mean to tap them but a rabbit shot across the road and his foot acted in reflex. Before he could turn with the skid the car slewed halfway around and almost to a stop.

The sheriff didn't bat an eyelash but Jonas could almost feel the rigidity in his legs, and after they had picked up speed again Hagenbaugh said quietly, "You haven't had any sleep either, remember. I couldn't even see that fucking rabbit."

Jonas didn't answer him. They had lost time and he could hear the rumble of the truck quite clearly now. He wanted to stay well ahead of it for a couple of miles yet.

But maybe he was too tired. Maybe he wasn't the driver he thought he was. He took the corners as fast as he dared, he kept the automatic gearshift in second and gunned his throttle on the short uphill stretches, but somehow the farting airblasting sounds of the log truck crept steadily closer.

"With a full load and eighteen wheels on the ground, what the hell do you expect?" said Hagenbaugh.

And then the road straightened out a bit where it overlooked the cloud-laden Sooska canyon, and there was the smoking stack of the log truck in Jonas's mirror once more, looming larger and larger. The driver laid on his horn; he seemed to be enjoying the chase.

"Well, pull over!" said the sheriff. "For Christ's sake, let the bastard pass—"

Hagenbaugh's voice stopped abruptly as he realized what he was saying. He sat motionless and silent while Jonas kept ahead of the truck for another half mile, until he rounded another corner, then suddenly braked and swung the car bouncing out onto the chewed up mud of the wider place on the shoulder, the place overlooking the steep rocky slope and the fog-bound river far below. The pursuing horn roared at them and over them, chips of bark flew past their windows, and the log truck splashed on out of sight.

They sat there for a long moment. Jonas noticed that his hands were wet on the wheel. "I guess the driver of a truck can see who he's *following*, all right," he finally said.

Jonas gestured to the bits of wreckage below. "Well, look at the file," he said. "Look at your own records. It *could* have happened that way."

SEVENTEEN

HE FELT AS THOUGH he had been driving forever. After taking the sheriff home Jonas went back to Burlington, where he got rid of the rental car and finally got a call through to Fred, in Seattle. Then for the third time that day he headed back toward the Sound and across the old causeway into Sooskamack. On an impulse, he stopped in at the Fish Trap, which was gathering the usual steam of men about to miss their supper, but he didn't see Tony Pedilla anywhere, and after some second thoughts and smells of the place Jonas decided not to ask about him. He was in no shape for such a meeting and maybe that was a card to keep in the deck for a while, anyway. With secret relief, Jonas put down his unfinished beer and left.

It was dark by the time he walked up the winding drive to the big house. It wasn't until he reached the worn brick parking area in front of the wide porch, slightly winded from his climb, that it occurred to him how automatically he had left the pickup parked out on the street again, just as though there were still turkeys in it. He smiled and straightened up as he rang the bell. Maybe he didn't have any hard evidence yet, but the hunches and theories were beginning to fit, a pattern was finally beginning to form. . . .

There was a rush of clicking steps and the door was jerked open. Louise Telford was startled, but then happy to see him. She still wore her elegant high-heeled boots and the suit she'd worn yesterday. "You just got back from Seattle," Jonas said. "I should have phoned, or maybe waited a little while."

"Oh, no," she laughed as she pulled him inside and swung the door shut. "I've been home for hours. The cook is gone today, so Clara is all alone. There are so many things to do, that's all. I was just on my way up to change. I didn't want to go shopping, that's all Adele ever thinks of. Anyway, it was raining in Seattle and I slip on the sidewalks. I never used to slip or fall when I was younger."

She led him past the stairway toward the sitting room where the painting of Myron was. "But I'm so glad heels are back in again. I just won't wear anything else in town. Yours are called duck boots, aren't they? Mack had a pair like that, he always loved them."

Jonas hadn't had a chance to change yet, either. He still hadn't had any sleep and it made her prattling words seem even more disconnected than they probably were.

"I hope you have a cat."

"What?"

"Cats adore leather bootlaces, didn't you know?"

"I could use one who likes mice," he said as he sat down, but she was already back on Seattle and the rain again. It was good to be here, he thought, and why had he bothered to ask the doctor if her mind was wandering? Of course it was, it was galloping all over the place. She was an old woman, for God's sake. She was delightful.

Then abruptly, "We heard about Mr. Johansen on the car radio," she said. "That was such a shock. I never really knew him myself, but I remember Myron always tried to find him extra jobs and Cal Simpson has done what he could to help. So have I, of course, with the man's poor sister—" She stopped with an uncertain glance at Jonas. "There wasn't anything you were going to tell me about his death, was there?"

He could hear sudden dread in her voice, see the flick of fear in her eyes. He wished he had a drink, but she hadn't offered him one.

"The sheriff is still investigating," Jonas said. "So far, all he knows for sure is that Johansen was shot yesterday morning, sometime before noon."

"Oh, how sad. And there we all were, praying for Emily—"

"It was earlier than that, probably. Like around the time when you were getting the church decorated."

"Oh, the minister and his wife did most of the arranging. But of course we'd planned it together, and I was up early cutting all the flowers and leaves and things right here. There were several carloads, it took us all morning, going back and forth, even with Clara and Marjorie Dunfield helping."

"Was anyone else here, helping?"

"Just Cal, with his car, that's all. He came before breakfast, a little before eight—and then Adele, of course, she came rushing to pick us up for the services, but that wasn't until almost noon. Why? Why do you want to know where people were?"

"Never mind. Let me ask you something else: Do you have any idea why Emily Stillwell might have wanted to visit Myron's old office, up in Telford? Was there anything she ever mentioned leaving there, or—"

"What? No, of course not. Why would she? I don't know what you're talking about." Louise frowned, trying to see into his eyes better.

"I just wondered, that's all."

"No, you didn't just wonder," she said, her voice rising. "You asked it. And I told you before, I have no idea what Emily could have been doing that day, or driving on that old road in Marjorie's car. But now, when we were talking about poor Mr. Johansen, you suddenly asked—"

"I know. Please, let's skip it."

"There's some connection, isn't there? You have an idea there's some connection between Emily's death and his—"

"All right, maybe I do," he interrupted firmly. "But until I can prove it—"

She pounced on his trace of uncertainty with relief, shutting her ears to any more. "Those stupid hunting accidents happen all the time around here, you know. In the old days everyone knew about guns, or we thought we did. But now they're just toys. And with all the drinking and drugs—when Mack got older, I used to beg him not to go hunting anymore. But what do you want me to do, he'd say, play golf for the rest of my life? Once I said yes and he never forgave me."

She was prattling to seal it, to make it be true, to postpone anything worse. It was kinder to interrupt. "Mrs. Telford, I also thought you might like to hear what I know so far about the girl."

"Oh, yes, the girl," she said, almost as though she had forgotten about Julie Mapes.

He told her what the queries from Hagenbaugh's office had yielded so far: Julie was known in California and Nevada, too, but there was no indication that she'd ever done anything criminal, not unless you considered running away from one orphanage and two foster homes crimes.

"No, I certainly don't," Louise said firmly.

"I wouldn't be too sympathetic," said Jonas. "She has also been lying about her age, apparently."

"Don't they all do that? To get drinks and things?"

"The dates on her IDs are altered, Mrs. Telford. She's really under age and that could get her in trouble, if anybody pushed it. She's a runaway from school right now, of course, and that's another count."

"But there are so many children like that, so many leave home, even the ones who have real homes!"

"I know, and some states would just as soon they never came back. Apparently nobody is screaming for this girl, but that's not the point. She's a phony, Mrs. Telford. She just has to be."

"Phony? What do you mean?" Louise seemed startled by the word. "How do you know, Mr. Duncan? Are there birth records or—"

"No, no, I'm just talking about the act Julie has been putting on. For instance, her hair isn't really that color."

"What?"

Louise looked confusedly toward the photo of young Myron that Jonas gestured to. She seemed fragile and frightened again. Jonas remembered the doctor's warnings. At least there was no point in confusing her with details of lab reports and stolen hairbrushes. He simply said, "We know she has dyed her hair."

"Oh, is that all!"

"Under the circumstances, Mrs. Telford, it obviously proves the girl's intent to mislead—"

She burst into laughter. "But everyone dyes their hair! You should see the hideous mousy gray mine is. And so thin, of course, but a permanent helps. Adele wanted me to have it done with more blue this time in Seattle, but I hate that. Anyway, I only had a set, I can't stand hairdressers. But you should see what color *Adele's* hair is! I can't think of a single woman I know who doesn't touch up one way or another.''

She was prattling again, evading, avoiding. Before, it had charmed him, now it was beginning to annoy him. Maybe he was getting too tired. Maybe she was. Maybe he ought to go.

She read his mind. "Oh, dear," she said, rising abruptly. "I know how exhausted you must be. Wouldn't you rather talk tomorrow? Yes, wouldn't that be better, if we talked tomorrow?"

Jonas stood up, feeling both relief and frustration. He could let himself out, he said. She started to say something more but then startled him by touching his cheek with her fingers instead, and turned quickly away to move up the stairway. Her trembling fingers felt even colder on his cheek than they had on his hand.

Jonas walked out through the hall toward the front door. There was soft music coming from the other end of the house, and as he paused to listen curiously for a moment he noticed that the door of a coat closet beside him was slightly ajar. There was something on the floor inside the closet that crowded the door. Jonas pulled the door wider open.

The thing on the floor was a lumpy rolled sleeping bag.

Angry nerves jiggled in his eyes as he strode through the big living room, then an empty formal dining room. The music grew louder; it came from the kitchen. It was rock music but not the noisy stuff, it was similar to the jazz he had heard in Cal's Lincoln last night.

He stepped into the kitchen. There was only Clara, at the sink, giving him a flustered, frightened look. To one side and closer was another swinging door that was still moving, and the music was moving in there, too. Christ, they were like belled sheep the way they dragged their drugging music around with them! Jonas slammed through the swinging door into a butler's pantry.

Julie Mapes whirled before she could reach another door, the tiny radio in her hand still mindlessly blaring.

"What the devil are you doing here?" Jonas said, reaching for the transistor.

"Don't!" she cried. "Give it back! That's mine!"

He was already snapping it off.

"They've got this great station up here, they play this neat stuff—"

"Where's your boyfriend? Where's Mert hiding, in the linen closet? The dumbwaiter?"

"The what? You get away from me! I didn't do anything."

"Answer me. Where is he?"

"Seattle, I guess. There's some guy he wanted to see about a job in TV."

"That guy moved out of town months ago. The sheriff has already checked."

"What? Well, I don't know anything about it. Let *go* of me!" He had barely touched her but she was shaking with panic. The skin of her arm was hard with goose bumps.

"What else don't you know? What other lies did you tell yesterday?"

"None! That's not so. Jeez, why do you hate kids so much?"

"I don't, Julie. I just hate JDs who try to rip off old people."

"I never!" she gasped wildly.

"Or con them, it's as bad as mugging—"

"No! You can't talk to me like that!"

"I have to, until you tell me the truth—"

"I know what's wrong," she suddenly, hysterically laughed. "You're just mad because I called you an old fart."

"Oh, for God's sake." He wanted to make her angry but his own anger kept interfering.

"Besides, Mrs. Telford says it's a' ..ght for me to be here. I told her I was curious about my father, is all."

"Your who?"

"Well, he *might* be. But that Myron Telford wasn't very much, everybody else around here says. Wouldn't you know. All your life you wonder what it would be like to have a father—"

"Julie, stop all this crap—"

"Stop it, both of you!" Louise Telford cried from the doorway. Her eyes were black diamonds.

Julie dashed past her into the dining room as though escaping from storm troopers. As he moved after her, Jonas almost expected her to say, "He's been beating me!" But instead she just whimpered, "I'm sorry, Mr. Duncan. Honest, I didn't mean anything bad. I didn't mean to call you names."

"Of course not, now that Mrs. Telford is here," Jonas said, grabbing firmly onto his own temper, trying not to see the frightened tears in Julie's eyes. "If you look closely at the girl's forehead, Mrs. Telford, you'll probably notice some red spots."

"What?"

"Tiny rashes, maybe even a few burn marks. When anyone changes their hairline that radically, the experts tell me, whether by pulling out hairs or using a depilatory—"

"What if I did?" Julie's hand flew guiltily to her distinctive widow's peak. "I told you, Mrs. Telford, I just wondered what I'd look like is all."

Louise Telford's eyes flicked from one of them to the other in a confusion of anger and fearful uncertainty.

"Julie is really a dishwater blond," Jonas said. "But of course yesterday she was careful to show the sheriff only a black and white picture from a newspaper, as though the color of your son's hair meant nothing."

"There's a color picture in a magazine, in the San Francisco Public Library, that's what I copied," Julie said quickly. "I already told her about it. Didn't I, ma'am?"

"Yes, she did, Mr. Duncan. There was an article several years ago in *Westways* magazine, about the history of the Telford family. One of the photographs showed Myron as a young man."

"There, you see?"

"How convenient," Jonas snapped. "And of course she knew she'd have to tell you that story in a hurry, Mrs. Telford, the moment she discovered her hairbrush was missing. Anyway, there was always the danger someone would spot the dye job. But not until after it had served its purpose and startled everybody."

"No! He makes it sound like—"

"Julie," he interrupted harshly, "just tell us who's been helping you. Is it only Mert, or is there someone else? Has someone coached you, helped you plan this whole thing?"

Julie burst into hysterical sobbing. "Oh, please, no, it's not true! It was just my idea, like I said. I wanted to know what it would be like, I was just curious—"

"All right, that's enough," Louise Telford cried. "Go to your room, Julia."

"Her *what*?" Jonas's outrage started to burst again but it was a wasted bubble. Julie was already in pathetic flight.

Louise Telford watched after the girl for a long moment, unable to look at Jonas. Louise's back was very straight, and when she finally spoke her voice was stiff and trembling. "I'm sorry, Mr. Duncan," she said. "I know you're really angry at me. I should have said she was here, but I couldn't. I guess I was afraid to. I was afraid of what you might say or do. But after Adele left here this afternoon, I found that child hiding beside the driveway, half frozen. I just *had* to bring her in."

"You should have called someone right then. The sheriff, me, your doctor—"

"A man, you mean. Well, this isn't a man's house anymore," she said firmly. "And the way you treat that child—"

"Mrs. Telford, I don't like it either. But I simply have to go on my experience with juvenile cases, with messed up kids."

"All right! I understand." Louise whirled and he saw tears sneaking into wrinkles that he hadn't even known were there before. "I don't blame you, I know she's probably lying, she may cheat and steal and take drugs, she may even be diseased. I know all those awful things. But don't you realize? If there really *were* such a person, such a daughter as my foolish son wished for, then what *else* would she be like?"

"I know," he said gently. "I've thought of that, too."

"Besides," she added shakily, "it isn't just the hair. There *is* a certain family resemblance—the eyes, the shape of her face—"

"But maybe that's exactly why she was picked," he interrupted. "Suppose someone chose her, put her up to all this. Maybe Julie herself doesn't even realize just how she's being used, or why. But the whole thing is simply too coincidental. Until we know the truth of how she fits in with Emily Stillwell's death, you just have to get her out of here."

"No," she said, pushing off his hands. "I've made up my mind. I'm going to satisfy my own curiosity."

If she were glass she might shatter any moment with trembling, but he had to risk it, he had no alternative:

"Mrs. Telford, I should have told you before: I *know* now that Emily Stillwell's death was no accident. I've finally figured out how she could have been killed."

"Well, for heaven's sake," Louise suddenly laughed. "You've been thinking that for days. Don't you realize I've seen you trying to hide it from me?" She started to move toward the living room, toward the front door.

"Listen to me," he said. "This is new. And it would mean Johansen's death was cold-blooded murder, too. So until we know all of it, know who the murderer was—"

"Exactly!" she cried with maddening finality. "That's exactly why I'm keeping the girl here. Until you know the whole truth, she'll be much safer, right here with me."

EIGHTEEN

THE LOG TRUCK chased him down the runway, but then disappeared when his sweating hands automatically awoke to tighten the seat belt. His stomach sank heavily for a moment while the plane climbed through streaming ink toward a startling, starlit sky. As the pressure relaxed, Jonas took a deep breath and looked around for the stewardess.

She was coming back into the aisle and she caught his glance. "I know," she said softly. "You're the vodka toddy." Other passengers were already asleep. The plane hadn't left Seattle until 1:00 A.M.

"Make it a double, will you?"

Maybe for a couple of hours, at least, he could stun his fears into oblivion. He was taking a chance, leaving Sooskamack, but it would be taking an even bigger chance not to, he had decided. When he last saw the sheriff, in the afternoon, Jonas had the uneasy impression that Hagenbaugh was still counting on his fingers, still rechecking each item in the files of his mind, still remembering on which side of the road he hadn't found any car tracks after the accident, still trying to decide if Jonas was right about the short time the bus driver and the TV repairman would have been on the county road before Johansen's truck came by—and therefore simply wouldn't have seen the sedan, not even if it was ahead of the truck by only half a mile or so. The sheriff stubbornly questioned whether Jonas had driven as fast as he could to stay in front of that guy he'd paid twenty bucks to, Bill Staples—and of course Jonas probably hadn't, he wasn't about to risk a wreck, but then neither had Staples really tried to run them down, for God's sake.

But even though the sheriff conceded that death *could* have come to Emily that way, still he obviously wasn't going to do anything about it for a while. When Jonas stopped by at his office after leaving Louise Telford's house, he found that Hagenbaugh had sent instructions from home that he was not to be disturbed under any circumstances.

Jonas went back to his motel room, but he was still too upset about Julie and Louise to go to sleep himself. Besides, there were overdue telephone calls to make. First to his police friend in Reno, who confirmed his earlier guess as to why the Blue Sage Detective Agency's telephone was temporarily disconnected: Nancy Snow, who only did occasional collections for local gaming establishments now anyway, had taken off a couple of weeks ago for a winter in Mexico and points south. Fortunately, however, there was a friend of the widow's in Carson City, a retired federal marshal named O'Malley, who had access to the Snows' files and records. O'Malley had just returned from an Arizona vacation himself and would be happy to cooperate with Jonas in any proper way. Jonas made a note of O'Malley's number and then called Northwest Investigators in Seattle. It took a little time but eventually he was informed that they were starting to check the names that Julie and Mert had given to the sheriff, in fact a San Francisco investigator had already contacted the most important one, the young mother of the baby with whom Julie had recently sat. She didn't have much to say, however; she had simply confirmed some of the things in Mert's statement.

It was then that Jonas decided to do his sleeping in planes and airports, decided to go after the facts himself. He couldn't risk half-answers or mistakes. He couldn't wait for the sheriff or anyone else.

Because if he was right about how Emily Stillwell had died, then even though her killing might have been hastily improvised, it was also cold-blooded and brutal. When Emily drove up from Portland, she must have gone straight to Telford, which was closest to the freeway. She had taken something from Myron's old office and then headed for Sooskamack on the familiar old road she'd used in the past; but Emily had been followed. She was chased by a log truck, and then she was dead. So regardless of exactly how the crash itself occurred, or exactly what the Swede's degree of guilt was, Johansen certainly would have known too much. He also drank too much—and so he ended up dead, too, in a second killing that was not only brutal but craftily planned as well. Like a chain saw in alder, the murderer was cutting in whatever way circumstance dictated, whatever way the wood might split. And having once killed, and killed again, it would be even easier to kill the next time. . . .

The stewardess brought his toddy and he asked her not to wake him up until the plane was unloaded in San Francisco. She gave him an extra pillow and he closed his eyes, but the Russian sleeping potion was little help. The moment he fell asleep, those hairy swaying logs came barreling back to tailgate his dreams.

At eight o'clock in the morning, he was met in downtown San Francisco by an earnest young man named Gilmore who worked for a company that had a reciprocal deal with Northwest Investigators. Gilmore was the one who had already contacted the girl with the baby, and he had a written report of their conversation that he planned to show to Jonas over a leisurely expense-account breakfast at the St. Francis Hotel.

"I'll read it in your car," Jonas grunted. "I haven't that much time."

The girl lived in the Marina district and said she didn't want to be bothered again, since she was just about to take her baby over to a friend's house while people came to spray her apartment for fleas. The outlandish excuse was probably genuine—fleas were one of the secret attractions of San Francisco, Jonas remembered. Anyway, she had already told Mr. Gilmore everything she knew on the phone, yesterday afternoon, so what else was there to discuss?

"Coffee," Jonas said, sitting down heavily in her most comfortable chair as though he intended to stay for a week. "I sure could use a cup of coffee."

"Now, look here," she started to object, but Jonas interrupted with a professional wink.

"That stuff in the station house is never any good," he said.

She stared at him. "I'll see what I can do," she mumbled, and walked out to the kitchen.

Gilmore cleared his throat. He didn't look happy.

"I told you I'm in a hurry," Jonas muttered quickly.

When she came back with the coffee she looked accusingly at Gilmore. "You said you were just a private investigator."

"Oh, he is!" Jonas said, before the young man could get his mouth open. "But we always cooperate on the big ones."

The baby started to cry in the next room. Its mother didn't even seem to hear. "What's so big about somebody just wondering who their family might be?" she asked nervously.

Jonas gestured toward Gilmore. "That's his problem," he said, sipping his coffee. "My only concern is with homicides."

"Homicides?"

She turned pale and abruptly sat down. Jonas couldn't look at her for a moment, nor even at Gilmore, whose face was turning red. Jonas was glad when the baby stopped crying of its own accord. Cop double-talk was a lousy trick but there was no time for anything else. He threw several rapid questions at the girl and her answers came anxiously fast. She had known Julie Mapes ever since seven or eight years ago when they were in the same orphanage together, though of course Julie was a lot younger than she. Julie was a good kid who never got in any trouble, except running away maybe, and everybody did that . . .

"But listen," the girl interrupted herself. "Julie's all right now, isn't she?"

"Of course." Jonas nodded. "But there have been a couple of unexplained deaths up north. I have to check every possible connection. Now, you mentioned somebody coming to see Julie at your orphanage, I believe. Years ago, some investigators came asking questions about her, something like that?"

The girl gave Gilmore a startled look. "I didn't tell you that."

"No, she didn't, Duncan."

"Is it true?"

The girl hesitated. "I guess so . . . I mean, sure, this man and his wife came and talked to a bunch of girls Julie's age. They had pictures to compare and they came back a couple of times after that."

"Do you remember what their name was?"

"Yeah. Snow."

"Lady's first name Nancy, I suppose?" Jonas said dryly.

"That's right."

"Quite a memory you have. What were you, maybe fifteen?"

The girl flushed. "Well, why not? Maybe I remember because the man was so crippled he had to use two canes. Or because the woman was so funny—sure, she *told* everybody to call her Nancy. She was big and fat and she laughed all the time and carried a whole candy store in her purse—"

"All right, then what happened?"

"Well, nothing! They just stopped coming, that's all. That's the way it always was. People would come asking questions about some kid, and see what she looked like, and the kid would get all excited, like maybe they'd bring a glass slipper for her to try on, the next time. Only people like that are just doing it for money, nothing ever really happens. Some kids are just suckers and dreamers, that's all." She checked herself worriedly. "Mister, what's that got to do with anybody being dead, up north?"

"I don't know yet," said Jonas, and switched back to the present. But the girl was rattled or scared enough now to correct some of the answers she had given to Gilmore on the telephone. For instance, it just might have been Mert who came after Julie so hot and heavy, instead of the other way around . . .

"What do you mean, hot and heavy," Jonas interrupted. "Are they lovers?"

"Jeez, *I* don't know. I don't think so. What do you want to know that for? It's none of your business."

Quite right, thought Jonas, and why in hell had he blurted out the stupid question? "She carries a newspaper picture in her wallet," he said quickly, "and she found another one in the library—"

"Sure, of that guy who Mert thought might be her father. Only Mert was the one who found that picture, I think. Or knew about it. Of course, I couldn't see much likeness myself. I don't think Julie did either, at first—only then just a week or ten days ago Mert found some more pictures someplace, and by then Julie was getting all excited—"

"Sounds like he did quite a job on her."

"Job?"

"On you, too, maybe. Mert claimed he was only in this by

accident. Said he'd met you and your husband last summer, so a couple of months ago, when he just happened to be down here from Tahoe, he thought he'd drop by and say hello. Only here was this baby-sitter, instead, who wanted to bend his ear about who she might be—"

"No, it wasn't that way," the girl interrupted quickly, embarrassedly. "Mert came looking for Julie."

"Then why didn't you say so? Why did you tell Mr. Gilmore—"

She lashed out with sudden anger. "Because that's what Mert asked me to say, that's why! Because it would help Julie's chances, he said—so I did it, that's all. For Christ's sake, I was an orphan too, you know. Julie was part of the only family I ever had, once."

"Take it easy—"

"Anyway, it was just ethics of the business, Mert said. Since it wasn't his case originally, there was no reason for people to know he'd ever been a private eye. And since Julie didn't even remember seeing him before—" She stopped as she saw the startled expression on Gilmore's face.

"Never mind him," Jonas snapped. "Go on."

"Oh, man," she said miserably. "You mean *all* us orphans are suckers and dreamers. Well, the first time Mert and I really met was six years ago, at that orphanage. He spent a lot of time talking and kidding with a couple of us older girls—oh, were we impressed! He let us sit in his car with him while his 'associates' went looking at the little kids—"

"The Snows."

"Yeah."

"What else?"

"That's all, until now. All I remember, anyway."

"Then what about now? Did he mention the name of anyone else who might be interested in finding Julie? Like someone up in Washington, maybe, or anybody in connection with those latest pictures he got? Even just the name of a hairdresser?"

She stopped shaking her head and suddenly laughed. "Oh, Mert claimed he was a hairdresser once, too. Wouldn't you know!"

NINETEEN

"HAIRDRESSER, MAYBE," said O'Malley. "Private eye, no."

"Did the Snows ever mention Mert's name to you?"

"Nope. But Nancy told me that when her husband got so crippled with arthritis she had to hire college boys as drivers, sometimes."

"That sounds more like," Jonas said. "Driver and bullshitter."

"Oh, Mert's a little more than that by now, maybe." O'Malley finished helping Jonas into a down jacket. "I stuck his employment record in the side pocket, there." He turned to stride through the wind toward a crowded stairway that led up through the airport terminal.

Jonas hurried up the stairway after him, suddenly feeling the altitude as well as the biting cold. It was just after noon when his four-propellered plane had crested the snow-clad Sierras and sunk into the smog of South Lake Tahoe. O'Malley, who turned out to be an elegant gaffer in cowboy boots and a mane of white hair, had met him on the field with the spare jacket tucked under his arm. Jonas was doubly grateful for it when they reached the parking lot and he saw that O'Malley's car was a battered Land Rover. They piled in and joined the steady stream of traffic on Highway 50, which rapidly became a clogged river the closer they got to the Nevada line. A few cars carried skis, Jonas noticed, but most were filled with the same faceless people who had overflowed his plane from San Francisco, the addicts who just couldn't wait to throw their money away on the dice and cards and slot machines.

"No, no," said O'Malley. "They only come here for the big shows and conventions, you know that."

"And the brown stuff at this end of the lake isn't sewage, I suppose."

"Hell, most of these nature-lovers don't even know there's a lake here. Some fine new condos and shopping centers, though. I tell you, South Lake Tahoe is getting almost as pretty as Las Vegas was, before they moved the city dump farther out."

And it used to be so beautiful, thought Jonas with an unhappy twinge, this lake ten times as blue as the sea, with that incredibly clear mountain air to breathe—and damn it, somewhere around that last bend, instead of wall-to-wall motels and parking lots, there was once a campground with plenty of space between the pines where a young cop and his bride could make love in a tent . . .

"The nickel slots," growled O'Malley from his own memories. "When they threw out most of the nickel slots for dollar ones they just ruined this place."

Jonas pulled the copy of Mert's employment record out of the jacket pocket. "Where'd you get this?"

"From a man I know, at the last place Mert worked. After you called me last night I did some nosing around. Found out where that cousin of Mert's is located, too, the one he borrowed the van from. Only that wasn't just because Mert needed wheels. He owns a Jag XKE that he's letting the cousin use for a while. Mert wanted something that looked more sincere, he said."

Jonas wondered how O'Malley knew all this, but O'Malley was way ahead of him. "Want to stop and see him, the cousin, I mean?"

"Where?"

"In that ten-story glass mausoleum coming up on the left. He's a blackjack dealer, in line to be pit boss. I told him I was looking for a second-hand Dodge van to fix up for rock-hounding. That got him going. He collects thunder eggs himself."

Jonas smiled. It was quite a fraternity he had joined by retiring early. There seemed to be useful ex-cops and frustrated detectives almost everywhere. "Do you think Mert told him where he was headed with the van, what he was going to do up north?"

"No, no, this guy's too willing to gab. Anyway, Mert's bright enough not to spill his own con, don't you think?"

"Maybe not. Taking a poke at my Indian friend was downright dumb, he could have blown everything right then. And these jobs he's listed, they're just the ones he told us about, they don't take any brains."

"But in all of them a guy gets to meet people, you notice? Rich people. Women. And somehow he's got that Jag paid for, and a little boat and a lot of fancy clothes, too, his cousin says. You ask me, Mert's one of those studs who just coasts until he spots an easy mark, a chance to latch onto something greener."

"He didn't put hairdresser on his job list, I notice."

"And spoil the muscle-boy image?" O'Malley suddenly tapped his brakes. "Hey, I know a gal runs a forty-hole beauty parlor back down the line. I bet she'd know something about him."

Jonas glanced at his watch. Their progress had been frustratingly slow past the huge hotels where shivering sidewalk crowds scurried endlessly from one golden casino to another. Trucks and concrete mixers choked the highway ahead, where even larger buildings were under construction.

"Never mind," Jonas decided. "Let's skip the cousin, too. Maybe this whole thing is simpler than I figured."

O'Malley took his foot off the brake, and in half an hour they had left the lake and the pines and were rolling down the long sagebrush slopes toward Carson City. The sage smelled sharp and clean, and Jonas noticed a new billboard beside the freeway advertising the Mapes Hotel in Reno. It wasn't a bad name for a lonely child to pick, he thought. At least it belonged somewhere, somewhere nice.

Nancy Snow lived in a freshly painted old farmhouse on an acre of blowing dust and cottonwood trees surrounded by barbed wire. O'Malley produced a key that let them in through a creaking side door to a barnlike room filled with machinery and piles of rocks.

"I thought it was her office we were going to," said Jonas, "not a gravel pit."

"This is how I met Nancy. She's in a club I go prospecting with sometimes."

"I'd hoped you were a little closer than that."

"Careful how you talk," said O'Malley. "Nancy weighs about two hundred and fifty pounds, not quite my style." He gestured to a littered workbench. "But her equipment is even better'n her jokes: three polishers, sanding wheels, imported diamond saws. Wintertimes I drop by for her, to make sure nothing gets rusty."

He led Jonas through a freezing hallway into a small room where there were a few wooden file cabinets and a rolltop desk. "Far as I know, this is the only office she's ever had. Nancy's half retired and the cases she does take are mostly for the casinos, running down welchers, bad checks, forgery, that stuff—and casinos don't want outside records kept anyway. But here." He twisted a key off his key ring. "She always says use my judgment if anybody really has to look at anything. I doubt if you'll find much, though. Just bad luck she took off before that girl popped up in Washington."

"No," said Jonas, "not luck. Mert probably waited to go north with the girl until Nancy was out of the way, that's all."

He turned to look through the file drawers while O'Malley fiddled with the desk. The Snows' old records were sketchy and elementary. Nancy was obviously more talker than writer. There was a folder labeled "Telford, general" that contained a few expense account records, several letters from Emily Stillwell, and even a note from Myron himself, thanking the Snows for some favor on a visit to Reno— but there was little that Jonas didn't already know. Behind that folder were two more, "Telford, photos" and "Telford, file copies." In the latter were yellowing carbons of letters to Emily, care of Telford Timber, referring to the search for Myron's mythical child, but none of them said much and some were apparently missing. "We'll send our summary report by next week," said one from several years back, but there was no further evidence of such a report. "Thank you for your nice phone call concerning our sad discovery in Boulder City," said another from the same era, but there was no other indication of what that discovery might have been.

The third file, "Telford, photos," was empty.

"You called it," said O'Malley. "No wonder Mert wanted to wait until Nancy was gone for the winter."

Jonas glanced at his watch. "I'll go try my own picture on the neighbors," he said.

The picture was a sketch of Mert that he had done on the plane from San Francisco, and apparently it had come out better than the ones he'd done of Julie. At least the first woman he showed it to recognized who it was supposed to be, and she made a face. Her first memory of Mert, she said, was shortly after Mr. Snow's death, when the young man showed up next door with some flowers, and then stayed for a while to be helpful as a handyman—until Nancy Snow caught him stealing or snooping or something and booted his ass out, and he left with the neighbor's hair dryer he was supposed to be fixing in the trunk of his car. That was a couple of years ago. Then just this last summer he showed up again, trying to make peace and butter Nancy up. Maybe he tried too hard, because several days before Nancy left she told the neighbor, "If you see that bastard once more, don't even tell him I've gone yet, just give him a load of buckshot!"

"*Did* you see him again? Like right after she left, maybe a week or ten days ago?"

The neighbor admitted she hadn't, she'd been away herself at the time. But that obviously only made it easier for Mert, who had plenty of opportunity to take whatever he wanted from the empty house. Anyway, Jonas had learned enough and now he was anxious to get back up north again. He hurried back to ask O'Malley if he would drive him straight to the Reno Airport.

O'Malley didn't answer for a moment. He was frowning over a ledger he had found in the rolltop desk. In it Nancy Snow kept a record of her income, which had dwindled to a few consulting fees from local casinos. But also, exactly one month ago, Nancy had received and deposited a personal check for five hundred dollars from Emily Stillwell.

TWENTY

"FIVE HUNDRED DOLLARS? How would I know what it was for? Settlement of an old bill, probably." Steven Argyle turned aside to shake off his spattered English trench coat while they waited for an express elevator. "The last time I spoke with Emily was shortly after Myron died, when we discovered what a mess his finances were in. She always worried about his reputation. I guess she was sore because I hadn't wiped up after him like she used to."

"Sore enough to hire a detective to prove you were wrong?"

"Don't be silly," Argyle smiled, his eyes on three jeweled Indian women in gossamer saris who waited for the same elevator. "There was no doubt about Myron's dipping in the till. You can see the private file at the bank, if you like. But at least it only added up to forty or fifty thousand dollars, and at least he cooled a couple of his roughest creditors by sending them checks, there at the end. Anyway, five hundred isn't much of a fee, it's probably nothing we're concerned with." Argyle's interest seemed elsewhere, as usual. When Jonas had arrived in Vancouver, he found that the lawyer was in a board meeting with Japanese and Canadian members; now he was on his way to an early dinner with some gentlemen from Beijing.

O'Malley, of course, would soon be getting answers to these questions from Nancy by phone. But just locating the freewheeling Nancy in Mexico might take several days and Jonas didn't have that much time. He had been away from Sooskamack for almost twenty-four hours, and it was making him more and more nervous.

144

The elevator doors opened and they were swept inside, crowded close to the clear plastic bubble that was the elevator's only outside wall. Jonas looked quickly up toward the top of the venerable Vancouver Hotel, a couple of blocks away.

"What's the matter," whispered Argyle. "Acrophobia?"

Jonas grinned, even as the wet street and tops of cars suddenly sank beneath his feet. "I suppose this is how you get your kicks," he said, "now you've given up high climbing."

Argyle laughed. "I still prune a tall tree sometimes or run up and down a telephone pole. It's better than jogging."

Jonas jerked his eyes away from the sloping roof of the Vancouver Hotel, which was opposite them now and sickeningly steep. The sky had been clear when his plane landed, but now there were fast-moving bits of cloud from the north, another weather front was moving in, and the elevator trembled in the wind. A woman gasped, a man giggled bravely, until at last they were safe in the shadowy elegance of a rooftop restaurant. It was crowded but the maître d' quickly recognized Argyle in his cashmere suit and led them toward a secluded booth. On one side Jonas could see the moving lights of aerial trams on Grouse Mountain, on the other were big ships coming in from Georgia Strait. In between and all around were the ghosts of snowy peaks so close you could touch them. But the clouds were gaining fast; soon even the endless carpet of city lights below would disappear.

"There are some other things I want to get straight," said Jonas, the moment they were alone. "Who would stand to gain by bringing that girl to Sooskamack?"

"Besides her and Mert, you mean? Nobody special, not that I can think of."

"So who would lose? The people who want Louise to give up her control of Telford Timber, I suppose, since Julie's presence might stall or delay things?"

"Oh, the kid could be a fly in their ointment, I guess. We've been over that."

"Yes, you told me before that Louise wouldn't budge until anything like this is all settled. But why is Chris Frame so bitter about Louise not letting go of the company sooner?"

Argyle shook his head and sighed. "Lord, who knows. In all the years he's pushed for more control, I've *quadrupled* the value of Telford Timber. By now his shares alone are worth four or five million. So what more does he want? To be his Uncle Mack? Times have changed. You've met Chris. He'll never make it. Not even in the woods," he added, smiling at the private afterthought.

"Is there anyone else who might be alarmed by Julie's showing up right now? Maybe some other possible inheritor—"

Argyle interrupted him firmly. "Duncan, there's something you may not understand. Even if this girl could prove she were Myron's real or legitimate daughter, a child has no inherent *right* to a parent's estate. Or a grandparent's, or any other relative's. If someone dies intestate, then of course that's a different matter. But that wasn't the case with Myron, and it certainly won't be with Louise."

"That's my next question. What's in *her* will? Where will Louise Telford's money go someday?"

Argyle hesitated, finally shrugged. "It's no big secret. Most of it goes to charity, a big endowment for the hospital, for instance. She already supports half of Sooskamack. When she's dead she'll keep on supporting it."

"How about relatives?"

"They're all mentioned, she's told everyone. Servants, old friends, they're modestly taken care of. No big beneficiaries, if that's what you mean. No secret heirs, no surprise bequests."

"But of course that could be changed if she took a sudden liking to this girl, Julie Mapes. So I suppose that might worry a few people."

Argyle smiled. "What makes you think Louise would ever do that?"

"Maybe she's already doing it," Jonas said. "Given the circumstances, how could *any* old woman, left all alone, *not* be intrigued by the thought of a possible granddaughter?"

"All right, but I'm sure when Louise hears what you've learned about Mert, she'll shoo the girl away and forget the whole thing."

"And I'm sure you know Louise Telford a hell of a lot better than that," Jonas said sharply, impatiently.

Argyle stared at him. "Duncan," he finally said, "have you one single bit of proof yet that Emily Stillwell's death was not an accident? Or that the Swede's death wasn't?"

"No," Jonas admitted, "not actual proof."

"Well, there you are. And you've certainly found nothing to suggest a big enough motive for two murders—hell, you're not even sure anybody besides Mert was involved in getting Julie up here."

"Damn. Is that the real world over there?" Jonas nodded in the direction of the elevator.

"The what?" Argyle looked to see three black-clad Orientals stepping into view. "Sorry. I guess they're early."

"It must be fascinating," Jonas said, "dealing with the high and mighty."

"Boring as hell, most of the time."

"Oh, but that's just one of the benefits, I suppose, that comes from handling big investments, representing big money. Power, influence, a base, whatever you call it—Telford Timber certainly must have helped you get where you are today."

"What kind of a crack—?"

"Oh, no offense. But when I asked who would benefit from Julie's being in Sooskamack, getting Louise all tied up with the family ghosts again, you forgot the one person who probably makes millions out of the status quo. You."

Jonas rose to go, feeling Argyle's dancing eyes on his back. But the lawyer jumped up after him, suddenly laughing and offering him a ride back to Sooskamack in the Rolls—if Jonas didn't mind waiting around in Vancouver for a couple of extra hours, that is. But Jonas did mind. He had stolen all the time he could spare, and at least he had a few more facts straight, maybe all Argyle would ration out tonight, anyway.

Turning down a ride in the Rolls might have been a mistake, however. It took Jonas longer than he expected to fly the short distance back to Seattle, then drive north again in his pickup, so it was almost midnight by the time he finally reached Sooskamack.

When he drove up Maple Street, he could see lights still on in the house on the hill. When he hurried up the drive it looked as if every room on both floors was lit. But no sound came from inside and in spite of the cold, the front door had been left open. He rang the bell, he tapped the knocker, he pushed the door wider open and called, "Mrs. Telford?"

No one answered.

TWENTY-ONE

JONAS STEPPED INSIDE and shut the door loudly behind him.

"Mrs. Telford?"

There was still no answer. He strode through the big dining room toward the kitchen, calling, "Clara?" But the kitchen area was empty and he hurried back toward the other end of the house, then stopped abruptly near the foot of the wide stairway when he heard a soft rhythmic clashing of metal from overhead. He moved rapidly up the stairway and along a hall until he could hear faint music playing beneath the louder clashing, banging of a cymbal.

He opened a door and for a split second ice touched his spine. There in a room filled with college pennants and road signs and record cabinets, seated behind a gaudy and glittering set of drums, was an old woman he could hardly recognize. Her face was buried in her hands, about all he could see at first was the stringy back of her neck stretching from her bathrobe as she rocked back and forth, her foot pounding a pedal in angry time with music from Julie's transistor, lying on the floor.

"Mrs. Telford!"

The cymbal gasped and died.

Jonas scooped up the little radio to snap it off. "Where is she?" he said. "What happened?"

Louise Telford stared at him with shocked, haggard eyes. "I'm sorry," she mumbled through white lips, trying to bring herself back from somewhere. "I'm sorry. I should have listened to you—"

"I asked you what happened?" Jonas interrupted more sharply.

She took a shaky breath, her eyes wandering sightlessly around the room. "We'd been having such fun all day, just talking and talking, looking at albums and the flowers in the greenhouse and playing Myron's records. Julie has quite a nice voice, you know. She has perfect pitch."

"Mrs. Telford, answer me!"

"I think there was a telephone call, Clara said. I was taking my bath. I knew I was getting too tired. What difference does it make? I should have known I would do it all wrong." She suddenly flushed and tears welled into her bloodshot eyes as memory came back, as angry shame and misery came back. "I've been a silly, stupid old woman."

"Where is Clara now?" Jonas said.

"That's exactly what Julie called me, and I don't blame her," she persisted. "After my bath I couldn't find her anywhere. I got much too upset, and when I did find her hiding in here, she said, 'Get away, you ugly old woman.' When I begged her to tell me what was wrong, she screamed at me." Louise's cheeks flamed with embarrassment. "She said, 'Leave me alone, you fucking old witch!'"

Jonas was already turning to run back toward the stairway. He had heard a door shutting, downstairs.

He found Clara frantically counting the silver in the butler's pantry.

"Stop that," said Jonas. "Where were you a minute ago? I called you."

"Down in the basement," Clara said, panting and counting at the same time. "That's where the liquor is kept, it was the very first thing I thought of, but none of it was touched, thank heaven. They'll take anything, you know."

"What do you mean, 'they'? The front door was open. Did Julie just leave here?"

"I heard a car screeching in the drive, it was that boy of hers in the van and he honked his horn and out she ran—that's all they do now, you know, just honk their horns—"

"Clara, what went on here?"

"Oh, for a time I thought everything was going to be all right. That girl even helped with the dishes, only then later she got a telephone call.

From him, I guess. Mrs. Telford was upstairs running her bath and I'd just taken her up some cocoa, so I couldn't listen. When I got back, Julie pulled the phone into a closet but I could tell she'd been crying and they were arguing, fighting. When she came out, I tried to ask her if I could help, but she wouldn't even look at me, and then she ran into the other part of the house. After a while I heard her screaming at poor Mrs. Telford upstairs. I guess she tried to stop her from leaving or something, because that's when the horn started honking and by the time I could run to help, she was already racing outside—"

"Clara, didn't you hear *anything* that Julie said on the phone?"

"Not really. But she did ask me afterward where Bayshore Road is."

"Where is it?"

"Down by the Sound. It's the one that turns off to go past the big sawmill."

The road was dark and deserted, it was unpaved in spots, and it skirted dangerously close to the steep banks of an inlet, but Jonas drove as fast as he could. The tide was full and the inlet was choked with logs in places, but he couldn't see far, the wind was slackening, the sky had filled with clouds. It was also freezing cold, driving with his window down, but he didn't want glass breaking beside his face if he missed a corner and hit a tree—or worse, hit empty space and the black water below.

Mert had at least a fifteen-minute start on him, and Bayshore obviously made a loop around a long peninsula, so Jonas might never catch up with the van. But it was worth a try. Wherever Mert and Julie were going, it wasn't for sight-seeing.

Several miles farther along the inlet he caught his first scent of the sawmill. It was a big one, all right, or once had been. He passed dark sheds and stacks of lumber and logs and a couple of places where forklifts and trucks and tractors were parked. He slowed down when he reached a lighted area where there were a couple of passenger cars and a pickup parked, but they probably just belonged to watchmen, since there didn't seem to be any work going on anywhere and there were no lights in the office buildings. Through the endless chain link fencing he couldn't see a single van, nor were there any cars at all on the other side of the road where overgrown railroad tracks ran out to abandoned pier-sheds. Farther on there were no more yard lights, just occasional black mountains of sawdust and the huge rounded cone of an ancient wigwam burner, one of the kind Jonas remembered from boyhood as flaming volcanoes whose sawdust sparks could light up whole miles of night. Now sawdust was a respectable member of the forest product family, and the burner was only a rusted skeleton.

After that there was no more fencing, just an occasional house or farm in the woods on one side and more logs and black water on the other. When he saw headlights approaching, the first he had seen since the mill, he slowed down. From the way it cornered and the shadows on the trees, the fast-moving vehicle could be a van, and though there might be a hundred other vans in the area, he blinked his lights and honked his horn as he swung sideways to a stop, partially blocking the road.

The other driver immediately veered in self defense—and sure enough, Jonas caught a glimpse of Lake Tahoe on the side of the Dodge as it skidded almost to a stop on the far shoulder.

Mert must have recognized Jonas's pickup at the same instant; he spun his wheels trying to get back on firmer ground, to get away, but then a door slammed open on the far side of the van and Julie jumped out. She was clutching something in her hand, but that was all Jonas could see, for Mert was already slamming on his brakes and leaping out after her, cutting her off. She ran back along the road as fast as she could go.

Jonas jumped out of the pickup to pound after them in his damn city clothes and bulky down parka. He caught a glimpse of Julie dodging into a side road, the entrance to a farm, but there was a fence and closed gate blocking her way, and she darted back across the road to a path that led down toward the water.

That was a worse mistake, for the path ended at a small floating pier, and by the time Jonas reached a place where he could see, Mert had trapped her on it. She was kicking and screaming as he tried to rip paper out of her hand. Jonas ran panting out behind them, slamming a blow into the small of Mert's back at least hard enough to make him let go of the girl, and she scrambled to the end of the pier while Mert whirled with a wild elbow jab into Jonas's stomach.

"Give it back," Mert shouted, "give me the rest!" as he leapt after Julie once more.

Jonas dived for his legs and the two of them went down in a tangle. As they rolled over, he saw that Julie had already jumped for the seeming further safety of the huge floating logs that snuggled close against the end of the pier. He yelled but it was too late to stop her, and Mert no longer cared to, he was already scrambling to his feet, looking more scared than anything else as he gave Jonas a final kick and turned to race back toward the road.

Jonas stumbled to his feet, tearing off his parka. He heard Julie gasp—she had run across several of the logs and was turning to look back when she obviously felt one of them moving under her feet. For a moment she froze.

"Run this way!" he called. "Run as fast as you can!"

But her weight had already made one log and then another start to rise and fall between her and safety. The log she was on suddenly started to roll and she jumped to the one beyond, but it was rotten. Her ankles sank below the surface of the water and she screamed.

Jonas tore off his suit coat and tugged at his shoes. "The end of the log, go to the end of that log!" he yelled. "It's clear water, run toward clear water!"

But even as he dove he could see her slipping, falling, and then the Sound hit his head like a block of ice. When he surfaced she had disappeared. But he could hear splashing and gasping, and he swam as fast as he could toward the sounds, then dove under logs until he caught a knee in his face. She grabbed wildly for him and he twisted her arm to shove her into a space between logs where they could gasp for breath. But the logs started moving back together again with enough force to crush a strong boat, so he blew the air out of his lungs and jerked her back down under water.

Julie wasn't much of a swimmer, but he could feel her trying not to lose control of herself, trying to obey his tugs and shoves and occasional gasped words. It took five more minutes that felt like fifty to work their way back to the protection of pilings beside the pier, and they had to cling there for another minute while Jonas tried to collect enough breath and strength to get them out of the water.

It was then that he noticed the wad of soggy paper she still clutched in one hand.

"What the hell is that?"

She couldn't answer, her shaking voice wouldn't work, and her fist was so cramped and cold that he had to help pry the fingers apart. What she held were the remnants of three greenbacks, three fifty-dollar bills.

"More," she gulped, "he—he had more," and then vomited the salt water she had been swallowing.

"Don't try to talk," he mumbled shakily as he wiped her face with his wet hand. With a surge of effort he hoisted himself out of the water and pulled her after him. Whatever marrow was left in his bones turned to jelly in the even colder air, and Julie's whole body started rattling. He found his down parka and shoved her arms into it. He grabbed up his suit jacket, which was no help at all. Julie started to rise but fell back. One of her knees was bleeding where her jeans were torn, and her hands were cut by barnacles. He took a deep breath and stooped to pick her up in his arms, expecting they both might fall down. But Julie was shockingly light, and she clung to him like a starfish as he stumbled across the pier toward the path.

"Somebody gave it to him," she chattered. "All that money."

"All right," he said. "Just hang on."

"He had some papers." Her voice was that of a very small child, shaking with fear of the dark and the cold. "He never told me until tonight. He telephoned, he said we had to go away, but we would get a lot of money."

"Who was he going to get it from?"

"I don't know. It was dark. He made me stay in the van. It was someone he met by the road."

"The same person he wanted to phone from the campground?"

"What?"

"That first night I saw you, he'd gone off looking for a phone, you said—"

"Oh, no, I don't think so. That's somebody he was mad at,

somebody chicken, he said, but he'd never tell me anybody's name or anything."

"Chicken," Jonas said, pausing to shift his grip on her. They had reached the path by now and in the distance he could see his pickup, but the van was nowhere in sight. Mert was long gone. Jonas resupplied his lungs and started plodding up the path.

"He said if I didn't leave with him tonight, they'd put me in jail."

"Why? What did he mean?"

Her shivering whimper was a try at a laugh but it came out more like a sob. "Because I'm no good. I'm all the things you said. I'm not Mr. Telford's daughter."

"What?"

"That's what was in the papers he had. It's true and Mert never told me before—I'm not Myron's daughter, I'm not anybody!"

She checked herself as Jonas abruptly stopped moving. He was almost at the top of the path and he could hear the soft sound of an idling car engine, quite close. Then headlights switched on, hitting them both in the face. The car was parked directly across the road, but from its angle he couldn't tell which way it had come from. Someone had been standing by the driver's side, and then the headlights swung away as the car roared off toward town. It was the Porsche. He couldn't see who was driving it, but the person hurrying toward them in slacks and a fancy fur parka was Adele Frame.

"My God!" she said. "Don't you know how short a time a person can live in that water? What on earth?"

"Shut up," said Jonas. "We've been practicing for a log-rolling contest."

"I'm sorry," she said quickly, touching his arm. "Your keys are in your pickup. I already looked. Wait here."

"I can manage," he mumbled and started to move along the road, but she was already running for the pickup and he was relieved to stop and lower Julie's weight for a moment. Adele Frame ran well, he noticed, and she handled the stick shift of the pickup like a stock car racer. He didn't argue when she insisted on driving.

"I've got to get the girl into the hospital," he said, trying to control his own shivering.

"It's too far, she'll go into shock. You're probably there already."

"I'm just fine," he said, fumbling with the heater control until she pushed his cramping fingers aside and twisted it higher herself. Julie was huddled between them, her face buried in his jacket, her spastic fingers clinging to his arm.

"We had just stopped there. I thought I saw someone on that old pier," said Adele.

"Who's we?" said Jonas. "And where are you taking us?"

"None of your business, and don't argue with me."

She gave the pickup a fast workout for another two miles farther on out the peninsula, then spun into a gravel drive that led to a big California-looking ranch house. She jumped out and ran to unlock the front door.

"Come on, Mr. Duncan," she called. "I'll get the girl."

But the trembling fingers still clung to his arm, and Jonas called back, "I'll bring her, I need the exercise."

"Men!" said Adele, leaving the door open and disappearing inside.

As Jonas hoisted Julie into his arms once more he suddenly realized that she had been crying.

"Hey, cut it out," he said. "You'll be okay."

"No," said her gasping small voice. "It's all my fault. I was so scared and mad—I was just awful—"

"Here we go." It was even easier carrying her this time.

"Is she all right?"

"Who?"

"Who do you think? She was so nice, and then I go saying those awful things."

"Oh. Yes, it wouldn't hurt if you cleaned up your act a bit."

"It's not an act!" she almost screamed.

"Your mouth," he said quickly. "That's all I meant."

They were inside the entry to the living room by then and he twisted to nudge the door shut. It was a huge living room that looked more expensively decorated than lived in. Julie giggled into his neck. "I don't notice your language is always so much." But the giggle turned into a sob. "I'll bet she hates me." The sob would soon turn into hysteria.

"Come on, get in here!" called Adele. "Hurry up!"

From somewhere behind Adele came the sound of running water. He followed her through a hall into Cleopatra's bedroom and from there into the largest bathroom he had ever seen. The deep shag carpet was warm with radiant heat, and steam rose above a marble bathtub big enough for three. "Jesus," he heard Julie mumble as he lowered her into a chair and Adele started pulling his parka off the girl. There were gold-framed paintings, Jonas noticed, hanging on the only wall that wasn't filled with mirrors. Paintings of nude women. "Supine," in the words of Cal Simpson. It was Edwardian barroom art of the very first water. "Tits like you never saw."

"Where did you get those?" Jonas asked. "Did Myron Telford leave them to you in his will?"

"Not exactly." Adele smiled. "But I'm sure he always wanted me to have them. Priceless, aren't they?"

"I'm sure."

"Mr. Duncan, I am trying to take this girl's clothes off and put her in the bathtub. Of course, if you'd rather do it?"

"Where's your husband?" he said. Julie was still hanging onto him, even while Adele tugged at her jeans.

"I haven't the slightest idea. But you can use his bathroom. It's through his bedroom on the other side of mine. Hurry up, before you catch pneumonia."

"I've had a pneumonia shot," he said, and gave Julie a reassuring pat as he scooped up his parka. "It'll be all right, honey," he said. "I'll be back."

"I'll be in there in a minute, to help you!" Adele called after him.

Like hell you will, thought Jonas. Things in Sooskamack were complicated enough already. There was a lock on the door between the bedrooms and he locked it. He picked up the phone beside Frame's properly spartan-looking bed and called the doctor, who didn't ask questions. He would do as Jonas asked. He would send an ambulance as quickly as possible. Julie would be put safely into the hospital for the night.

Next he called the sheriff, who agreed to put out an immediate all-points for Mert and the van. Then Jonas went out to his pickup and got the boots and jeans he always kept behind the seat with his parka. He went back into Frame's bedroom, found a bottle of brandy, and took it into the bathroom, where he stood in Frame's shower like a defrosting mackerel until he stopped shaking enough to put on one of Frame's wool shirts. He was surprised to find that it more than fit. Frame didn't give the appearance of being that big.

He called into the other bathroom to make sure Julie was all right, and Adele insisted he take a look for himself. He did and she was, and the moment the ambulance arrived for her, Jonas piled into his pickup and headed full speed for Sooskamack.

TWENTY-TWO

THE FISH TRAP was about to run down for the night. The earlier high tide had receded, leaving a stranded flotsam of pool addicts and wife haters and poor fish who were unable to swim home alone. The air was rancid with too much smoke and old stories told too many times. Only the hardiest of survivors still supported the bar. Among them was Tony Pedilla.

By the time Jonas parked his pickup in the dark street he was over his chills, but his exhausted lungs still ached and there were pains in his bruised shoulder and the leg where Mert had kicked him. When he hurried from the warmth of his car into the even thicker warmth of the tavern, the chills came back again, for he saw Pedilla almost immediately among the several men who looked curiously toward the cold draft of his entrance. The others stared at him for an unfriendly moment, but Pedilla turned quickly back to the bar. He was drinking beer, Jonas noticed, and he had a shot glass beside it. Jonas moved to a place farther down the bar and ordered scotch, paying no attention to Pedilla, and after a few minutes the place drifted back to its normal discordant noise level.

Jonas drank the scotch, took a deep breath, and strolled along the bar as though headed for the men's room. Pedilla was arguing with someone, not paying attention, and Jonas saw his opportunity. He stepped close and put his hand on Pedilla's right arm, near the elbow.

"What the hell?" The elbow jerked loose and Pedilla's beer sloshed on his pants. But he forgot about it when he saw whose hand had touched him. "Watch it, for Christ's sake!" he blustered, turning back to the man on the other side.

Jonas took another deep breath. The arm was enormous, and it had the right lump in the right place. Pedilla was the guy, all right.

"Watch what?" Jonas said quietly. "My wallet?"

Pedilla broke off his conversation on the other side. He turned to stare at Jonas through bloodshot eyes. "Mister, I don't know what you're talking about. Just go away, will you?"

"Care for another?" the bartender said hastily to Jonas, trying to gesture him back toward his empty glass.

"No, thanks," said Jonas, not moving, and then softer, to Pedilla, "Relax. You just owe me some money, that's all. I got the wallet back."

"Buddy, I toldja, get lost!"

"Do you want me to say it louder?"

"Mac, you're making a mistake," said the bartender, reaching for Jonas. "Better leave him alone."

"What I said was, you owe me some—"

"For shit's sake, Danny, go wash your dishes!" Pedilla roared at the bartender. "Everybody talks at once in here."

The bartender retreated.

"Exactly what I say," said Jonas after a moment. "Maybe we'd better go outside."

Pedilla stared at him. "Yeah," he said with a sudden laugh. "That's a good idea." He laughed louder. "That's a hell of a good idea!"

Jonas followed him toward the back of the room.

"Where you going, Tony?" someone called, and a couple of others started to rise as though they might tag along, but Pedilla laid a heavy arm over Jonas's shoulder. "To show this guy where the can is. Anybody follows me gets pissed on."

It seemed to work; no one followed. They went out past the toilet and kitchen and storeroom into a dark alley. Before Pedilla could make a move Jonas ducked out from under the arm and whirled. "Where's the sketch pad?" he said, trying to keep the shivering out of his voice. "That book with the drawings in it?"

"Mister, I don't know what the fuck—"

"Oh, shut up. Two nights ago, you broke into my motel room. You assaulted and robbed me."

"Jesus Christ, of all the crazy—"

"But all you took from my wallet was the cash, in hopes it would look like a kid or a junkie had done it, right?"

Pedilla didn't answer. He was swaying slightly on his feet, but it was too dark to see what was happening on his face.

"And the sketch pad? Well, maybe a kid might keep that, there were drawings of pretty girls, or a girl and a woman—but the trouble is, Pedilla, I can prove it was *you* who took it."

"Look, you son of a bitch—"

"So who put you up to it? You're a cat driver, for Christ's sake, or you are when there's work; you're not a mugger—"

"What's going on out here?" The sharp high voice was that of Chris Frame. He had just stepped outside from the Fish Trap.

"Nothing! Not a damn thing, sir," Pedilla said quickly. "It's all right."

"Like hell it is," said Jonas. "Join the party, Mr. Frame. I didn't notice you, inside."

"I just stopped by for a nightcap. Tony, what's he talking about?"

"You know damn well," said Jonas. "The other day outside the church, you told me your wife had been pumping Clara about me, just that same morning. That's how you learned why I was in town, you said. From gossipy Clara. That's how you learned about the girl, Julie Mapes, and what she looked like."

"Well, Clara is a fine woman," Frame said stiffly. "I'm sure 'pumping' isn't exactly—"

"But Clara was busy all that morning, helping Mrs. Telford and Cal Simpson with flowers for the church, and your wife didn't even get over there until just before noon, just barely in time to pick them up for the memorial service. Anyway, you were out all morning looking at some timber, you said. So when *did* you learn I was here to check on the girl?"

"Well, I might have been mistaken, maybe Adele said something the night before—"

"Or maybe you saw a couple of stolen sketches, right? Oh, not that anybody knew I'd have them. I'm sure you just told Pedilla to find out what he could about me, maybe you didn't even expect him to break into my room—but at least from those sketches of Julie you could have added two and two—"

"Sketches? I don't know what you're talking about." Frame was ashen, motionless.

"The guy's nuts, don't listen to him!" Pedilla whirled to yell at other men who were peering out the back door of the Fish Trap now. "You bastards stay outa this. Go back inside!"

But they didn't move and Jonas was shivering again. He knew he had to get this over quickly. "Mr. Frame, you also told me that morning you'd pay anything to get rid of Julie, to get her out of town. Well, how much did Mert charge you, tonight?"

"Did what? Who? I won't answer that." Frame looked even more shaken and confused. Behind him men were starting to step outside, trying to hear better. Somewhere close the brakes of a car sounded.

"Oh, yes, you will," Jonas said. "You'll also show me what Mert gave you in return—some papers or something about the girl—because otherwise, I'll tell Hagenbaugh what Pedilla did for you, maybe what you hired him to do. I'll see that he's charged with assault and robbery—"

"He's lying!" Pedilla yelled frantically. "I'll break his damn neck!"

"No you won't, you sonofabitch." Frame's voice was shaking, his face suddenly livid.

They both lunged at once, and Jonas was in the middle. He started to step back when a hasty hand from behind gave his arm a jerk that made him trip and fall to the ground. It was Cal Simpson, who had come running from a sheriff's car parked at the end of the alley.

But Jonas needed no rescuing. Frame's murderous blows were all aimed at Pedilla, while the bigger man blocked as best as he could and lunged frantically to get away. By now, however, the other men from the Fish Trap were piling into the melee in righteous support of the town's biggest employer, in gleeful vengeance against one of its louder bullies. Pedilla went down fast, and not even the yelling of Al, the deputy sheriff who came running from the car after Simpson, could be heard in the pandemonium.

But Jonas was still just hearing Frame's last hysterical words: "You son of a bitch, filthy bastard—she said a maid gave her those sketches—"

And Pedilla's frantic pleading, "No! I didn't do nothing, it was just a favor—honest, Mr. Frame, I never touched her! Never! Jesus, I'm no Filipino!"

"I'll be damned," said Jonas to himself.

"What?" Cal Simpson was staring aghast at Frame's shocked rage as men tried to pull him back.

"Never mind. Cal, what are *you* doing here?"

"Oh, Al saw your pickup, we been looking for you. See, him and me have a beer sometimes after he gets off duty, only when I stopped by the sheriff's office, this message was coming in, Mr. Hagenbaugh was already taking off—"

"Why? What message?"

"Somebody spotted a van with a picture on its side."

"Where?"

"In the drink."

TWENTY-THREE

IT LAY EMPTY on its side in fifteen feet of water and it was Mert's van, all right, as a wet-suited diver soon confirmed. The driver's door was unlatched.

It had happened at a place near the beginning of Bayshore, where the winding road first skirted the steep banks of the inlet. There was nothing unusual that Jonas might have noticed when he drove past here earlier, even if he hadn't been concentrating on not sliding off the road himself. The ambulance attendants who drove out to get Julie and take her to the hospital hadn't seen anything, either, said the sheriff. There were a few tracks and skid marks to be examined, but no broken glass or scarred trees indicating the van had crashed before sailing over the edge. Actually, it might not have been discovered for days or even weeks if an Indian gill-netter working close to shore hadn't heard the heavy splash and got curious with his searchlight. It was he who had radioed the sheriff's office.

Jonas watched a heavy tow truck back into position near the edge of the bluff. "Just keep them off those tracks we're marking," Hagenbaugh called to Al. A second assistant was leading Cal Simpson and other hastily deputized men in beating their way with flashlights through the brush and driftwood along the shore.

"Not that they'll find anything, or anybody," the sheriff grumbled. "You want to bet Mert just sent his own buggy over the edge—threw it in gear and jumped?"

"Maybe," said Jonas.

"Well, after tangling with you and losing a few of those fifty-dollar bills, not to mention the girl, he must have figured half the state would be looking for him. The van isn't worth much, he'd know that crazy picture on it would get him caught in five seconds."

"Maybe," said Jonas.

"Maybe, hell! It's less than half a mile from here to the main road to town. With a little luck getting rides, Mert would be in Canada by now!"

The sheriff went off to supervise the tow truck while Al piled into his car to go after a statement from the Indian gill-netter, who had been asked to tie up at one of the old sawmill piers. Jonas decided to join him.

They found, however, that the fisherman hadn't seen or heard anything to even suggest there was a man in the water or ashore anywhere around the sunken van. He had just assumed there was a body down there, and now was disgusted with himself for losing all this time from setting his nets. If somebody only dumped that car to get rid of it, then he damn well expected a piece of the salvage rights.

By the time Al and Jonas got back, the van had already been tugged up against the rocky shore. Before Jonas could start down for a closer look the sheriff intercepted him.

"Don't waste your time," said Hagenbaugh. He gestured toward a big car parked behind the litter of vehicles now lining the road. "Somebody else wants to get this over with." It was Chris Frame's Cadillac. "Just listen to him, that's all. And take it easy, for God's sake. He has his own problems, you know."

"I've met some of them," said Jonas.

Chris frame was pale and tight-lipped, his former wrath shrunken to cold sarcasm. As Jonas climbed in beside him he snapped on a lantern to augment the overhead light and handed Jonas a copy of a letter.

It was one of two Xerox copies of carbons, obviously taken from the files of Nancy Snow, which Frame said he had purchased from Mert tonight. Frame had already, voluntarily, shown the letters to Hagenbaugh, he said—though he didn't give a damn whether that impressed Jonas or not; he just didn't want anyone's overgrown curiosity giving him piles.

The letter was dated several years ago, addressed to Emily Stillwell and signed by Nancy Snow. It concerned the sad discovery that she and her husband had made in Boulder City, Nevada. According to musician correspondents of the "young woman from Telford," that's where she was at the time when she was telling Myron she was in a hospital having a baby. But none of the letters to her friends mentioned any pregnancy, and a check of hospitals in Boulder City revealed that the only babies born there of transient mothers, anywhere near the proper time, were four boys and one Vietnamese girl. No locally born baby had been put out for adoption during that entire quarter. The Snows were satisfied that any further search for the mythical child would be a waste of time and money; they were finally convinced that Myron's daughter simply didn't exist.

Jonas shrugged. "What else?"

Frame handed him the second letter, a copy of an earlier report summarizing visits that the Snows had paid to various western orphanages in search of close-dated births or look-alikes. But in each case there was some discrepancy, some wrong factor that canceled the child out as a possibility. Opposite the name Julie Mapes was the notation "wrong date, wrong location; left on church doorstep w/ bottles, blanket, etc, est. age already 3 mos., in Bishop, CA."

Wrong everything, thought Jonas, case closed. "I'm not anybody," Julie had said.

"You don't seem very surprised," said Frame.

"I'm not," Jonas sighed. "Obviously Mert wouldn't have tried so hard, he wouldn't have fiddled around with her hair and all, if he weren't already convinced she was no Telford. What did you pay for these things?"

"I gave him five thousand dollars in cash I got from the bank late yesterday afternoon, plus a ten-thousand-dollar cashier's check. I told the sheriff he can verify that if he wishes."

"Why only fifteen thousand? You would have paid more than—"

"I certainly would not. This is nothing but quick insurance, that's all. To protect all of us from unscrupulous lawyers, from the vagaries of an old woman. But also to protect her. Because I made Mert promise to get the girl out of here. I didn't give him the money until I knew she was with him and they were on their way. Only then, of course, you had to interfere."

Jonas reached for the door handle, but Frame was quickly conciliatory. "Duncan, you won't prefer charges against Pedilla, will you? The poor man has six children to support. Though, naturally, if you were injured, whatever you feel your loss was—"

"You'd be happy to buy my silence. I understand."

Frame flushed, went stiffly on. "I've spoken with my wife. I'm sure it was Pedilla's own stupid idea, breaking into your room like that. She may have mentioned your name, he's been out grading our road lately. He'd seen you with Argyle, knew other people were curious about you. The damn fool simply wanted to make points with me, I suppose—"

But Jonas was already getting out of the car. He had heard quite enough. He stomped down the dark road and promptly bumped into Hagenbaugh.

"Well?" said the sheriff.

"Charlie was sure right about the crawly things. So let's all cover them up again quick, right?"

"Huh? What's the matter, don't you believe Chris Frame? Believe those letters? Don't you believe the girl is nothing but a phony?"

"Oh, of course I do, and I don't give a damn about Pedilla."

"Then what are you sore about? At least *that's* cleared up."

"Sheriff, why did Mert settle for peanuts? With Louise Telford so interested and Frame so eager, he could have made a fortune out of that girl and you know it. So why did he suddenly decide to cut and run? What scared him? *Who*?"

"I'm sure when we find Mert—"

"What makes you so sure you will? Anyway, could Mert tell you what Emily Stilwell was doing up here in the first place? Tell you why she was killed on that road on her way to Sooskamack, or why the Swede was killed, or why Emily hired Nancy Snow again—not years ago, just weeks ago?"

"Oh, there I'm one jump ahead of you. You didn't think I'd wait for your old buddies to get in touch with that lady detective, did you? I've already got our senator to put pressure on the Mexicans to help locate her, we'll be talking to her too, in no time—"

He trailed to a stop as Jonas suddenly turned away from him to glare up into the heavy black sky. The wind had died.

"That's not good enough either," Jonas said quietly after a moment. "A few hours, maybe, that's all we've got left to find *anything*. Keep your crew here working fast and give me a radio, I'll be in touch—"

"Huh? What are you talking about?" The sheriff suddenly jerked off his hat. Something soft touched his face. "Oh, shit!" he said.

It was starting to snow.

TWENTY-FOUR

I T S N O W E D off and on through the remaining brief hours of the night, first in soft splashes and then in white powder that drifted with the wind. By eight-thirty, when the morning sky finally reached the color of wet cement, there was a thin white blanket over the chewed up, frozen mud of the road shoulder where the blue pickup was parked. The branches of trees in the Sooska canyon below were already well dusted; in sheltered places near logs and rocks the snow was several inches deep.

Jonas sat in his pickup with its motor running and the heater turned high, waiting for someone to show up in response to his latest radio message. His boots were wet and his feet were numb with cold, for he had been there more than two hours, first tromping around with a flashlight, then without it, then just tromping now and then to keep from freezing. He remembered to open a window slightly, and didn't use the windshield wipers too often to scatter snowflakes, because they kept clicking too much like a clock, clicking, clocking, clicking . . .

"Wake up!" shouted Al the deputy, jerking the door open so fast Jonas almost fell out.

"For Christ's sake," he grunted, "I'm all right."

"Sure you are," said Cal Simpson, catching an arm to help him stand up straighter.

Not one but two sheriff's cars had apparently sneaked up on him, Jonas noticed. As he shook himself awake and walked over toward

169

Hagenbaugh, who sat listening to his radio and adjusting the plastic cover on his pretty white hat, a third car came into view. A Cadillac.

"Look who tagged along," said Al. "He won't go home. It's giving the boss fits."

"What I want to know is what *I'm* doing here." Simpson was shivering. "A guy could freeze his balls off!"

"You're still deputized, buddy, so suffer."

"I need your help, Cal," said Jonas. "But there's a bottle in my dashboard. Both of you help yourselves."

While the two men hurried back toward the pickup, the sheriff snapped off his radio and kicked his door open. "Negative, negative, negative," he snapped. "Not a sign of him anywhere. Oh, but I know, you're not surprised!" He got out of the car to button up his sheepskin. "So what's the big hurry? What do you think we're going to find up here?"

"Well, while I was waiting for you, I spotted all sorts of animal tracks, the little ones, the burrowers, the weasels—"

"I know, and when the varmints get worried, that means we're in for it. This whole canyon could be buried in snow and ice for the entire winter. So you're a weatherman, too."

"At least I've finally figured out a few things. Anyway, this is our last chance to discover any real proof of murder."

Hagenbaugh looked haggard. "Duncan, I hope you also realize this whole case is maybe blowing up on us. And if it does, this whole town is going to blow up on me. There's just no way that dumb business with the girl could have been a motive for even a single killing—"

"I know. It makes things a lot simpler, doesn't it?"

"No! I spent two hours up here myself yesterday, just looking for Emily's keys, and all I got for it was bruises on my butt from falling down on all those rocks. How you'll find anything now there's mud and snow—"

"You just didn't look in the right place." Jonas checked himself as he heard the faint squeak and clink of approaching snow chains. A moment later the Rolls swung into view and crunched to a stop beyond the pickup. Steven Argyle, elegant in a Russian fur hat and fur coat, stepped out from behind the wheel. Adele Frame, even more elegant in arctic fox, stepped out on the other side.

"Oh, Lord," the sheriff muttered. "How'd *they* get here?"

"I thought you might like a witness or two," said Jonas.

Frame was already out of his car, staring at his wife. "What are you doing with him?"

"Why, darling, I thought you might need a lawyer. Besides, I wanted to tell Mr. Duncan how clever I think he is, with his little pencil." She waved Jonas's sketch pad briefly before tossing it back into the car. "Oh, but I wouldn't want your girlfriends to get snowed on, Mr. Duncan. Who's that older one, by the way? I hope you're not angry, I really do like art—"

"Adele, be quiet. I've taken care of all that."

Jonas didn't say anything. Argyle had already moved closer and touched his arm.

"You woke up a banker, I'm told," the lawyer said quietly.

"That's right. To look up the listing of Myron Telford's last checks. There were several more than there were canceled checks up in his old office."

"Well, they didn't total much. And there was only forty or fifty thousand spread over more than a year that he took from the wrong funds."

"Sure, let sleeping dogs lie. And when I asked you what that five hundred was that Emily paid Nancy Snow, you said settlement of an old debt, maybe. Don't you think it was more likely a retainer for something new?"

Argyle didn't answer, and Jonas moved back toward the pickup with the sheriff close beside him.

"Oh, boy," Hagenbaugh muttered grimly, "I just hope you know what you're doing!"

"What do you want *me* for?" said Simpson as he and Al hopped out to join them.

"There's something in the locker in back there. Bring it along, will you, Cal?"

Cal scrambled into the back of the pickup and lifted the metal lid of the locker. "Christ almighty," he gasped. "Where'd you get a fingernail cutter like this?"

"I borrowed it. Let's go."

"Here, I'll help," said Al, reaching over the side of the truck for the chain saw that Simpson lifted into view. It was a big one with nearly a four-foot bar, and the sight of it startled even the sheriff.

Jonas led the way down the steep slope into the canyon. His bruised leg was unsteady and he stumbled but managed to avoid falling. Chris Frame hesitated, then moved curiously after them, glancing back now and then toward his wife, who stood motionless, watching from above while Cal Simpson awkwardly eased the big saw down over slippery rocks with the deputy's help. Only Argyle had no trouble with the descent, never taking his hands out of his pockets as he slid and jumped downward until he was past them and almost out of sight in the swirling clouds of powder snow that shrouded the remains of Marjorie Dunfield's car.

"Over here, Al," said Jonas, moving to the place where the big Douglas fir log had torn up the earth, then rolled peacefully on for another hundred feet to rest against the dwarf pines. Beyond were the ghosts of trees and rocks that bordered the lower canyon of the invisible river.

Jonas gestured to the Douglas fir. "I want you guys to cut this log, right about there."

"Sure," Al said, putting the saw down on a flat rock, checking its chain tension.

"Hey, Mr. Frame?" Cal Simpson panted. "You know that's one of our own sticks? So maybe you'd rather—"

"What of it? For Christ's sake, you old nanny, give him a hand. Let's get out of here!"

"Yes, sir." Simpson's red face turned even redder. "You're the big fucking boss." He spat on his hands, reached for the saw, and jerked its cord hard enough to disembowel a chicken.

Jonas stepped back beside Hagenbaugh who stood watching from the shelter of a large rock. "Well, where else could you safely hide anything around here?" Jonas muttered to the sheriff. "There must have been a peavey on the truck; the log could have been prodded and rolled a little, to cover a few things up.''

The saw sputtered and choked and spat blue smoke. Simpson jerked it again and again, sweat pouring down his face.

"You're flooding it," snapped Frame. Adele was coming down the hill now, he noticed, taking her own graceful time. "Here, damn it, I'll show you." He angrily flipped the choke and braced the saw to tug its cord with even more vicious strokes.

Simpson moved uncertainly back toward Jonas, wiping the sweat off his face. Jonas reached out his hand. "I hope you didn't kill the whole bottle."

Simpson grinned as he produced the now half-empty pint of Southern Comfort. "You remembered, didn't you? Ambrosia, that's what Myron used to call it." He stooped to scoop the oversized bottlecap full of the snow, then poured the sweet liquor over it and handed the icy cup to Jonas. "Hallelujah!"

"Amen." Jonas downed the drink and turned to the sheriff. "I wonder if that old man at Skookum Corners ever got his cougar," he said.

The sheriff stared toward the log. "Jesus Christ," he whispered. "Is *that* where you found the varmint tracks?"

"It's the only place I looked."

The saw sputtered and died again. "Give me that damn thing before you wreck it," said Argyle. He picked up the saw with one hand and bounced its starter cord like a yo-yo with the other, until the motor finally caught for good and its roar filled the canyon. He raced it for a moment, then let it drop to idle as he took a running jump up onto the log. "If I cut it here, that end will twist downhill past the pine, okay?"

Jonas nodded and Argyle started cutting in the back side of the log. Adele in particular seemed hypnotized by the loose way Argyle handled the saw, like a butcher knife. But its roar was deafening, and Jonas took the bottle out of Simpson's hand as they moved behind the big rock where it was quieter.

"Cal, something's been bothering me. You used to have a blue pickup like mine, you said. You and Myron took trips in it, sometimes. Like to Frisco or Reno for the chips and chippies."

"Sometimes."

"Is that why Mert tried to look at my registration? Because he thought it was your car?"

Cal stared blankly at him. "I didn't know he did. I don't know what you're talking about."

"Well, you must have known him, or at least have seen him once or twice, in the past. He drove for the Snows, and Myron checked in with them a couple of times, didn't he?"

"Oh! I didn't even connect at first. Yeah, I remember who the Snows were. I guess Mert might have known who I was."

"So are you the guy he was mad at for turning chicken?"

"For what?"

"Didn't you have anything to do with bringing the girl up here, and maybe change your mind?"

"Christ, no!" Cal roared. "Do you think I'd do anything to hurt Mrs. T? If somebody was in on that with him, it sure as hell wasn't me!"

"All right, skip it."

"I love her, for God's sake, same as I did Myron."

"I know. The sweet simple guy who played drums and drank too much. You had all those wonderful times together."

Cal reached for the bottle but Jonas kept hold of it. Cal was already stumbling more, Jonas noticed.

"And everywhere you went, I suppose, he signed another check, or gave you money to pay a bill, and you put it in your pocket instead."

"That's a goddamned lie! I didn't—"

"Or maybe you just signed the checks yourself. In the last year, I noticed, his handwriting sure went downhill."

"You're full of shit! Give me that bottle."

Jonas gripped it more firmly. "Get your hand away or I'll break your nose with it."

The sound of the saw dropped abruptly to its idling growl and Jonas took a step back to see that Argyle had finished his slice in the back of the log and was now considering the front. Cal Simpson took an angry step after Jonas but stopped when he saw the sheriff strolling closer.

"Listen," Cal said. "I heard Mr. Argyle himself tell Mrs. T it was only forty or fifty thousand—"

"Oh, I'm not so worried about that money. But six months ago, someone else might have been really upset by all that skimming. Cal, did Myron Telford himself discover that you had your hands in his pockets?"

Simpson's head was shaking, his whole body shaking. His hand fumbled against the loose rocks beside him.

"Did your best friend catch his best friend stealing from him—and maybe the shock even helped him into his stroke?"

The chain saw blasted again. Argyle was making a deeper slice in the front of the log, to make the short end swing cleanly downhill a few feet without either splitting or pinching his saw.

Cal shouted wildly to make himself heard. "You're crazy! I wasn't even here then. Myron sent me off the day before to deliver a couple of checks, to pay a couple of bills—"

"Oh, I know that's your story. But did anyone see you go? Did you only deliver those checks to his roughest creditors, or did you also *write* them, maybe, and use them to buy yourself an alibi? There's somebody else who could have figured that out, you know. So is *that* why Emily came up here? Did her detective friend discover things at the casinos that made her realize you'd forged those checks *after* Myron died? Did Nancy Snow suspect you might even have killed Myron? Tell me what happened, Cal—did Myron just fall down those stairs after he had the stroke, or did you push him?"

Cal roared as he swung a heavy rock. Jonas was already sidestepping, getting a foot in his way, and Cal crashed heavily to the ground.

The sheriff had his gun out, but Cal couldn't get beyond his hands and knees. He was being sick at his stomach.

"Christ, I thought you were just looking for papers here, missing checks, something Emily took from those files at the shingle mill," said the sheriff.

"I know," said Jonas. "Some of this may sound like guesswork. But I finally figured out the simple reason for the craziest puzzle of all—

why Emily came up here in that big borrowed car instead of her own handy small one. It was because she'd brought somebody with her."

"Look out!" Chris Frame yelled. There was a cracking sound from the bottom of the log as its shorter end started swinging and skidding downhill, revealing what had been buried beneath it. . . .

"Oh, my God," said Argyle.

The heavy log, which had kept only the bigger critters away, was slowly scraping what had once been a huge fleshy arm off the nibbled and worm-crawling corpse of a very large woman.

"Nancy Snow weighed two hundred and fifty pounds," Jonas said softly.

TWENTY-FIVE

" I ' M S U R E H E didn't mean to kill Myron. My son did have a bad heart, you know." Louise Telford spoke in little more than a whisper, her eyes roaming over a tea tray that needed no attention.

"I know." Jonas glanced at his watch. He wanted to make the five o'clock ferry but she had insisted on giving him tea. She had insisted on knowing everything, no matter how it shocked or hurt or confused her.

"But the point is, *Cal* knew he had killed him. He had also met the Snows; he knew what Nancy's business was. So when he pulled into the mill yard with Johansen and saw a strange car, and then Mrs. Snow coming out of Myron's office with Emily Stillwell, it was like the sky caving in on him. Mert had told him that Nancy was on her way to Mexico—oh, yes, they had been in touch, I was sure of that—and obviously it was because of nosy Mert that Nancy let everyone think that's where she'd gone. For six months Cal had thought he'd got away with everything, thought he was in the clear. Anyway, when the women were obviously afraid of him and took off in a hurry, Cal ran back to the Swede's truck—they'd been out drinking together all day, the Lincoln was having its valves ground—and he pushed Johansen over and took off after them."

"Cal was driving that truck?"

"Of course. Oh, he still claims he just wanted to stop them, to talk, to reason with them—but it was perfectly obvious that Nancy had caught on to what he'd done, or would soon enough, so when he finally overtook them, you know what happened. The Swede was hurt, but Cal worked all alone for hours to not only hide Nancy's body in the only way possible down there but also cover her grave with something heavy enough to keep the larger animals from ever digging it up, ever exposing the remains."

"Do you know," Louise said softly, "I always rather liked Cal Simpson."

Jonas glanced quickly at her. She was sitting very straight, but her skirt was twisted and she didn't notice it. Her hair needed combing. A light had dimmed somewhere; too much had happened.

"I've got to be going," he said, starting to rise.

"Oh, no, wait. There's something I want you to tell the sheriff. I simply don't know how Cal could have caused Mr. Johansen's death. You see, that morning when we were getting the flowers ready for the church, Cal brought his car over here very early—"

"I know, before breakfast," Jonas interrupted. "And Johansen's sister didn't get the call from her brother on CB until eight-thirty. But the Lincoln not only has CB but a tape deck with a recording head, too. The Swede made plenty of calls to his sister. Cal simply copied one the day before, when he was getting more worried about Johansen's drinking and possible loose mouth. Then he just played it to her from right here in your driveway, and gave himself another alibi, after the fact, after he'd already killed Johansen earlier that morning. Mrs. Telford, Cal may have been a good man, once, but people turn into something else when they murder, and then think they have to keep on murdering. That's what Mert must have begun to suspect about Cal, I guess, and it scared him enough to cut and run—but Mert never made it. Cal intercepted him and killed him, too."

"Oh, no!"

"I was pretty sure of that when Cal was so emphatic about not having been in touch with Mert, when they obviously had been. He could say anything he wanted if he knew Mert was dead. He's out showing deputies where he dumped Mert's body right now, in a different arm of the bay. I'm sorry. That's how the world is, these days."

Jonas rose for good this time. Mrs. Kelly was expecting him for supper. There would be lovely fresh snow on the island. There was seldom any crime there.

"But your son didn't steal any company funds, Mrs. Telford. He wasn't a thief."

"Oh, but I let everyone keep thinking it! Emily had more faith in him than I did."

"I'm sorry . . . I've got to go."

"Please, what about Julie? Steven Argyle told me what was in those letters, he was very nice about it."

"I know. He was even nice to me when I woke him up at six o'clock this morning to borrow a chain saw. But Julie is out of the hospital. She's perfectly all right. So who knows? By now, she could even be running away again."

Louise didn't smile. "She forgot her radio."

"I know."

It wasn't easy to go, but he left in a hurry. The moment the door was shut she would probably start crying, for Myron, for Nancy Snow, for Emily and the Swede and even Cal Simpson—and he was a coward, thought Jonas, but his work was done, he simply couldn't stay.

He trotted down the drive and across the street to the pickup. He opened the driver's door, and there on the far side, clutching her rucksack and sleeping bag, sat Julie Mapes.

"Where the devil did you come from?"

"Mr. Hagenbaugh dropped me off."

"What?"

"He said you might be in a hurry. He said you probably wanted to catch a five o'clock boat."

"Oh, he did?"

Her mouth seemed dry and she talked very fast. "He said it was all right, because I mustn't go too far away for a while, because they'll want me for some more statements or maybe even the trial. But the islands are right close, he says, and I can't get lost there. Sometimes there are even jobs a kid can get, he says—"

"Now, wait a minute!"

"Please, Mr. Duncan, I won't be any trouble, honest I won't. I swear I'll never do a dumb thing like jumping on logs again in my whole life."

"You sure as hell won't! What did you tell the sheriff, anyway?"

"Well, he sort of understood it would be all right with you, I guess. He knows you're gone quite often, so maybe you could use a house-sitter sometimes—"

"Oh, no, you don't."

"Please, Mr. Duncan, I'd go to school, I'd clean house, I'd do anything. I always wanted to live on an island."

He could feel anger rising, or was it panic? She was talking like a ten-year-old but he kept remembering how she looked in the bathtub last night. My God, did fathers have trouble like that? "Julie, you can't do it. It isn't right. People who live on islands—well, it's not the real world, that's all. Christ, there aren't even any bears out there."

"Wow! Really?"

"Honey, people need bears to grow up. You've done just great, so far. You can't run away . . ."

He stopped abruptly as he heard steps hurrying across the street behind him. It was Louise and she hadn't been crying, in fact her skirt was straight and her hair looked better and the shawl she had thrown around her shoulders was made of silver, not ashes.

"What on earth?" she said.

The moment Julie saw Louise she started to sob. "Oh, Mrs. Telford . . ."

"I noticed you from the window. Julie, what's the matter?"

"I . . . I . . ." She couldn't get any words out, only tears. For her too much had happened, too.

"Come on, get out of there. You'll make Mr. Duncan miss his ferry."

"What?"

"And stop that silly crying. Now, hurry up. Come on."

Julie skidded quickly across the seat to jump out of the pickup. "Why? Mrs. Telford, I just thought maybe I could—"

"Never mind, we'll talk about it later. Here, take your knapsack . . . Well, don't just stand there, you'll freeze to death. Get back in the house. Scoot!"

Julie looked hesitantly from one of them to the other. Jonas didn't say a word. She suddenly turned to run up the drive and out of sight.

Louise Telford drew a shaky, determined breath. "I don't care if there's a resemblance or not," she said. "I don't care who she is. Of course, I realize I was never much of a mother before; it was probably my fault, what Myron became—"

"Your son, Mrs. Telford, simply was what he was. A likable guy who loved music and gambling and girls who played with toys—"

"Oh, yes, he loved all the wrong things. He made his father angry even when he was tiny, just for playing with dolls, and of course I let him pick out the wrong one."

"What do you mean?"

"Raggedy Ann instead of Andy. He kept it hidden in his room for years. I don't know what ever became of it. But maybe I've learned a few things in all those years, and if Julie could use just one or two of them—?"

There was pleading in her voice, but Jonas was suddenly handing her the lumpy sleeping bag and stooping to kiss her cheek. He jumped into the pickup and headed for the causeway and the road to the ferry landing as fast as he could go.

And Kathy was beside him, laughing and crying with the seagulls.